Charlotte Mary Yonge

Sowing and Sewing

Outlook

Charlotte Mary Yonge

Sowing and Sewing

1. Auflage | ISBN: 978-3-73261-954-2

Erscheinungsort: Paderborn, Deutschland

Erscheinungsjahr: 2018

Outlook Verlag GmbH, Paderborn.

SOWING AND SEWING.

A Sexagesima Story.

BY

CHARLOTTE M. YONGE.

New York:
E. P. DUTTON AND CO.,
39, WEST TWENTY-THIRD STREET.

PREFACE.

PERHAPS some may read allusions to a sacred Parable underlying this little story. If so, I hope they will not think it an irreverent mode of applying the lesson.

C. M. YONGE.

SOWING AND SEWING.

CHAPTER I.

THE SERMON.

Four girls were together in a pleasant cottage room with a large window, over which fluttered some dry sticks, which would in due time bear clematis and Virginia creeper leaves.

Three of them were Miss Lee's apprentices, and this room had been built out at the back of the baker's shop for them. The place was the property of the Lee family themselves, and nobody in Langley was more respected than they were. Ambrose Lee, whose name was over the baker's shop, and who kept a horse and cart, was always called Mr. Lee.

He had married a pretty, delicate young girl, who had soon fallen into such hopeless ill-health, that his sister Charlotte was obliged to live at home to attend to her and to the shop. And when young Mrs. Lee died, leaving three small children, another sister, Rose, gave up her place to help in the care of her old father and the little ones.

Rose Lee had been a sewing maid, and, being clever, had become a very fair dressmaker; so she took in needlework from the first, and when good old master Lee died, and the children had grown old enough to be more off her hands, she became the dressmaker and sempstress of the place, since there was no doubt that all she took in hand would be thoroughly well turned out of hand, from a child's under garment up to Mrs. and Miss Manners's dresses. "For," as her sister Charlotte proudly said of her, "the ladies had everything made down here, except one or two dresses from London for the fashion." Her nephews were both from home, one as a pupil-teacher, the other at a baker's with a superior business, and her niece, Amy, the only girl of the family, had begun as a pupil-teacher, but she had such bad headaches at the end of her first year that her father was afraid to let her go on studying for examinations, and cancelled her engagement, and thus she became an assistant to her aunt. Then Jessie Hollis, from the shop, came home from her aunt's, unwilling to go to service, and begged Miss Lee to take her and teach her dressmaking; and, having thus begun, she consented, rather less willingly, to take likewise Florence Cray from the Manners Arms, chiefly because she had known her mother all her life, and believed her to be careful of the girl; besides which, it was a very respectable house.

As plain work, as well as dressmaking, was done, there was quite enough employment for all the hands, as well as for the sewing machine, at which

Amy, a fair, delicate-looking girl, was whirring away, while Jessie was making the button-holes of a long *princesse* dress, and Florence tacking in some lining; or rather each was pausing a little in her work to answer Grace Hollis, Jessie's sister, a businesslike-looking young person, dressed in her town-going hat and jacket, who had stepped in, on her way to meet the Minsterham omnibus, to ask whether Miss Lee wanted to have anything done for her, and likewise how many yards of narrow black velvet would be wanted for the trimming of her own and Jessie's spring dresses.

Miss Lee was gone up to the house for a grand measuring of all the children for their new frocks; but Amy began to calculate and ask questions about the width and number of rows, and Jessie presently said—

"After all, I think mine will look very well without any round the skirt."

"Why, Jessie, I thought you said the dress you saw looked so genteel with the three rows——"

"Yes," said Jessie; "but I have thought since—" and she hesitated and blushed.

Amy got up from the machine, came towards her, and, laying her hand on her, said, gently—

"I know, Jessie."

"And I know, though you wanted to keep it a secret!" cried Florence. "I was at church too last night!"

"Oh, yes, I saw you, Florence; and wasn't it beautiful?" said Amy, earnestly.

"Most lovely! It is worth something to have a stranger here sometimes to get a fresh hint from!" said Florence.

"I call that more than a hint," said Jessie, in a low voice. "I am so glad you felt it as I did, Flossy."

"Felt it! You don't mean that you got hold of it? Then you can tell whether it was cut on the bias, and how the little puffs were put on!"

"Why, what are you thinking of, Flossy?" exclaimed Amy. "Bias—puffs! One would think you were talking of a dress!"

"Well, of course I was. Of that lovely self-trimming on that cashmere dress of the lady that came with Miss Manners. What—what are you laughing at, Grace?"

"Oh! Florence," said Amy, in a disappointed tone; "we thought you meant the sermon."

6

"The sermon?" said Florence, half annoyed, half puzzled; "well, it was a very good one; but——"

"It did make one feel—oh, I don't know how!" said Jessie, much too eager to share her feelings with the other girls, even to perceive that Florence wanted to go off to the trimming.

"Wasn't it beautiful—most beautiful—when he said it was not enough only just not to be weeds, or to be only flowers, gay and lovely to the eye?" said Amy.

"Yes," went on Jessie; "he said that we might see there were some flowers just for beauty, all double, and with no fruit or good at all in them, but dying off into a foul mass of decay."

"Ay," said Grace; "I thought of your dahlias, that, what with the rain and the frost, were—pah!—the nastiest mess at last."

"Then he said," proceeded Jessie, "that there were some fair and comely, some not, but only bringing forth just their own seeds, not doing any real good, like people that keep themselves to themselves, and think it is enough to be out of mischief and do good to themselves and their families."

"And didn't you like it," broke in Amy, "when he said that was not what God asked of us? He wanted us to be like the wheat, or the vine, or the apple, or the strawberry, some plain in blossom, some fair and lovely to look at, but valued for the fruit they bring forth, not selfishly, just to keep up their own stock, but for the support and joy and blessing of all!"

"One's heart just burnt within one," continued Jessie, "when he bade us each one to go home and think what we could do to bring forth fruit for the Master, some thirty, some sixty, some an hundredfold. Not only just keeping oneself straight, but doing something for Christ through His members."

"Only think of its being for Christ Himself," said Amy softly.

"Well," said Grace, "I thought we might take turns to go to Miss Manners's missionary working parties. I never gave in to them before, but I shall not be comfortable now unless I do something. And was that what you meant about the velvet trimming, Jessie? It will save—"

"Fifteen pence," said Jessie.

"Very well—or you may say threepence more. So we can put that into the box, if you like. I must be going now, and look sharp if I'm to catch the bus. So good-bye, all of you."

"Oh! but won't you have the self-trimming," broke in Florence. "Perhaps she'll be there on Friday night, and then we might amongst us make out how

7

it is done."

"Florence Cray, for shame!" said Grace. "I do believe you minded nothing but that dress all through that sermon."

"Well," said Florence, who was a good-humoured girl, "there was no helping it, when there it was just opposite in the aisle, and I'd never seen one like it; and as to the sermon, you've just given it to me over again, you've got it so pat; and I'll go to the missionary work meeting too, Grace, and very like the young lady will be there, and I can see her trimming."

"If you go for that, I would go to a fashion-book at once," said Grace; "but I must really be off now, I've not another minute to stop."

"Oh dear, I forgot," cried Florence, jumping up, "I was to ask you to call for our best tea-pot at Bilson's. And my mother wants a dozen—" and there her voice was lost as she followed Grace out of the room through the shop, and even along the road, discoursing on her commissions.

Amy and Jessie were left together, and Amy stood up and said:

"Dear, I am so glad you felt it as I did!"

"One could not help it, if one listened at all," said Jessie. "Amy, I must be doing something for His sake. I can't rest now without it. You teach at the Sunday school. Don't you think I might?"

Amy meditated a little.

"I think they would make up a class for you. When Miss Pemberton's niece goes away, the class she takes has to be joined to her aunt's, and that makes a large one."

"Then will you speak to Miss Manners for me?" asked Jessie. "Are they little girls or big ones?"

"Oh, that's the second class. They would be sure not to give you that," said Amy, as if she thought the aspiration very high, not to say presumptuous. "Perhaps Margaret Roller, the pupil-teacher, you know, may take that. Then I should have hers and you mine. They are dear little girls, some of them, only Susan Bray always wants a tight hand over her, Polly Smithers is so stupid, and Fanny Morris is so sly, one always has to be on the watch."

"Here she comes," said Florence, who was the nearest to the window, and the entrance of Aunt Rose, a brisk, fair little woman, young looking for her age, recalled all her "young ladies," as Florence and Jessie, and perhaps Amy likewise, preferred being called, to recollect that stitching was, at that moment at least, the first thing to be attended to.

CHAPTER II.

THE SUNDAY SCHOOL.

Perhaps Amy's business-like tone about the school classes fell a little flat upon Jessie's ear. She had not been to a Sunday school in her childhood. Her father had been a prosperous upholsterer's foreman in Minsterham, and Grace and Jessie had gone to an "academy" till, when they were sixteen and fourteen years old, their father died of a fever, and their mother, who had a cottage of her own at Langley, resolved on coming back and setting up a small shop there for all sorts of wares, with Clementina Hollis over the door.

Jessie was about eighteen, two years younger than her sister. She had always been a bright, quick, lively girl, but never very thoughtful, and much too inquisitive, till her curiosity had brought on her a terrible accident, which had kept her laid up in a hospital for many weeks. She had come home quite well at last, and much improved. A fellow patient, and likewise a lady who had visited her and lent her books, had both made much impression on her. She cared about right and wrong as she had never done before, was more useful at home, and tried to restrain her inclination to find out all about everything; she said her prayers more carefully, went to Church more often, and heeded more what she heard; and altogether she was what her mother called an altered girl. This was Lent, and a clergyman was staying with Mr. Somers to preach a course of sermons on the Friday evenings, and it was one of these that had so much struck these young girls, and had put into their minds for the first time, with any real force, the full sense that the true Christian must seek to work for the good of the household of Christ as well as his own household, and that "bringing forth good fruit" does not simply mean taking care of oneself, and trying to save one's own soul.

The language had been beautiful and stirring, and there was a burning desire in more than one heart to be doing something for Christ's sake. The first thing that Jessie thought of was the Sunday school. She had read books about it, and her fellow patient was full of ardour about "training little lambs," as she called it, so that it seemed the most beautiful and suitable task she could undertake.

Amy Lee, on the other hand, hardly knew how to spend a Sunday without the school. She had been a scholar there until she had quite outgrown the first class, and had been more than a year confirmed, and then she had become a teacher of the little ones. She liked the employment, and was fond of the children; she would have been sorry to drop the connection with Miss

Manners or with Miss Joy, the mistress, and the rest of the school staff; she was pleased to work for and with Mr. Somers and Miss Manners, and she had been trained to be reverent and attentive; but it had never occurred to her to think of it as more than a nice and good thing to do, or to look on it as a work undertaken for Christ's sake.

"Teaching at school, I do that already," she said to herself, when Aunt Rose's entrance had made her work her machine more and her tongue less. "I must get something more to do. Oh! I know. There's poor old half-blind Mrs. Long. She is left to herself terribly, they do say, and I'll go and tidy her up, and see to her and read to her every day. I could do it before my work and after. Maybe I might get her to be a better old woman than she ever has been. Books say that nothing so softens an old woman as a nice, bright young girl coming in to make much of her, and I'm sure I'm nice and bright—not so much in myself, but compared with the whole lot of Longs."

So Amy told her plan to her aunts, as soon as Florence and Jessie had gone home to dinner.

The two aunts looked at one another, and Aunt Charlotte said, "Did the sermon make you think of that?" in rather a doubtful tone.

"Yes," said Amy. "One seemed to long to be doing some good, not be only an empty flower, as he said."

"Mrs. Long," said Aunt Rose; "she ain't a very nice person to fix upon."

"But no one wants it so much, aunt," said Amy.

"That's true," said Aunt Charlotte. "Well, Amy, we must think about it, and speak to your father. Run out now, and gather a bit of parsley for his cheese."

Amy knew it was to get her out of the way, and felt rather disappointed that the proposal was not seized upon at once, and applauded.

"She's a good girl," said Aunt Rose.

"Well, so she is, and I don't like to stand in her way," said Aunt Charlotte.

"But to pitch on old Sally Long of all folk in the world!" said Rose.

"There's no doubt but she does want something done for her; but I misdoubt me if she will choose our Amy to do it. Besides, I don't like her tongue. That's what daunts me most."

"Yes. If she took it kind of the girl, she would never be satisfied without talking to her of all the old backbiting tales that ever was! And we that have kept our girl up from hearing of all evil just like a lady—"

"What is it?" said Ambrose Lee, himself coming in, after putting up his cart.

"Why, that sermon last night has worked upon our Amy, so that she wants to do something extra," said Aunt Rose.

"A right down good sermon it was," said the father; "a bit flowery, to suit the maidens, I suppose."

"And she said it all off to me, quite beautiful," said Rose, who had stayed at home.

"And what does the child want to be doing? I won't have her go back to her books again, to worry her head into aching."

"No, that's not what she wants. Her notion is to run in and out and see to old Widow Long."

"Widow Long!" exclaimed the baker. "Why, she's got as slandering a tongue as any in the parish! Give the poor old soul a loaf or a sup of broth if you like, but I'll not have my girl running in and out to hear all the gossip of the place, and worse."

"I knew you would say so, Ambrose," returned Charlotte. "All the same, the child's thought shames me that I've never done anything for the poor old thing; and she won't harm me."

Ambrose chuckled a little. "I don't know but aunt likes a spice of gossip as much as her niece. 'Tis she tells us all the news."

"Well, I can get plenty of that in the shop, without going to Dame Long for it," said Charlotte, laughing. "I like the real article, genuine and unadulterated."

They were laughing at Aunt Charlotte's wit when Amy came in, and she looked from one to the other, afraid they were laughing at her project, and ready to be offended or hurt. She did not like it when her father said, "Look here, my girl, Aunt Charlotte says Dame Long's dish of tongue is too spicy for you, and she must have it for herself."

"I don't know what you mean, father," said Amy, nearly crying, "I didn't want it for that."

"No, you didn't, child," said Charlotte; "but come along here, I want you to help me dish up."

Amy came with the tears standing in her eyes into the back kitchen, vexed, angered, and ready to be cross. Her aunt set her to prepare the dish for the Irish stew, while she said, "Father was at his jokes with me, Amy. He don't

13

like you to be running in and out to old Sally Long by yourself; no more does your Aunt Rosy nor I; but the poor old body didn't ought to be neglected, and the sermon was just as much for me as for you, so I've made up my mind to look after her a bit, and you may come in with me sometimes if you like."

"That was not what I meant," said Amy, rather fretfully.

"I dare say not. There, mind what you are about, or you'll have that dish down. Where's the flour? Come, now, Amy, don't be daunted, if you can't do good quite in your own way; why shouldn't you ask Miss Dora now?"

Amy muttered and pouted. "I'm not such a child now!"

"Ain't you then, to be making such a pout at not getting just your own way."

Down came the dish with a bounce on the table, and away ran Amy up the stairs, where she cried and choked, and thought how hard it was that she should be hindered, and laughed at, and scolded, when she wanted to do good, and bring forth the fruit of good works.

She heard Aunt Rose ask where she was, and her Aunt Charlotte answer, "Oh! she will be down in a minute."

She felt it kind that no one said that she was in the sulks. The relief did her good; she could not bear that any one should guess what was amiss. So she washed her face in haste, tidied her hair and collar, and hoped that she looked as if she had gone up for nothing else.

Perhaps her father had had a hint, and she was his great pet, so he took care that the apprentices should not suspect that Amy had been "upset." So he began to tell what had made him late at home. He had overtaken poor Widow Smithers in much trouble, for she had had a note from the hospital to say that her little boy, Edwin, must be discharged as incurable. It was a hip complaint, and he could not walk, and she had not been able to find any way of getting him home.

It so happened that all the gentlefolks were out for the day, and she did not get her letter in time before the market people set off. She was indeed too poor to hire a conveyance, and was going in, fearing that she might have to carry this nine-year-old boy herself five miles unless she could get a lift. So Mr. Lee had driven her into the town, and after doing his work there, had come up to the hospital, and had taken her in with poor little Edwin, who was laid on a shawl in the cart, but cried a good deal at the jolting. The doctors said that they could do no more for the poor little fellow, and she would have to take him home and do the best she could for him.

It fell very hard upon her, poor woman, for she was obliged to go out to work every day, since she had four children, and only Harry, the one who was older then Edwin, earned anything—and indeed he only got three shillings a week for minding some cows on the common. The two girls *must* go to school, and indeed they were too young to be of much use and the boy would have to be left alone all day, except for the dinner hour, as he had been before the hospital had been tried for him.

"There, Amy," said Aunt Charlotte, as they were clearing away the dinner things after the menfolk had gone out, "there's something you could do. It would be a real kindness to go in and see after that poor little man."

"Yes," added Rose; "you might run in at dinner time, and I'd spare you a little time then, and you might read to him, and cheer him up—yes, and teach him a bit too."

"Edwin Smithers was always a very tiresome, stupid little boy," said Amy, rather crossly, from her infant school recollections.

"Then he will want help all the more," said Aunt Rose, and it sounded almost like mimicry of what Amy had said of old Mrs. Long.

She did not like it at all. It is the devices of our own heart that we prefer to follow, whether for good or harm, and specially when we think them good. And yet we specially pray that we may do all such good works as our Lord hath *prepared for us to walk in*, as if we were to rejoice in having our opportunities set out before us, yet the teaching a dull little boy of whom she had had experience in the infant school, did not seem to her half such interesting work as converting an old woman of whom strange things were said.

However, Amy was on the whole a good girl, though she had her little tempers, and did not guard against them as she ought, thinking that what was soon over did not signify.

By and by, Jessie came back radiant with gladness, and found a moment to say, before Florence Cray came in, that her mother was quite agreeable to her teaching in the Sunday school, if Miss Manners liked it. She had gone there herself for some years when she and Miss Manners were both young, and she was well pleased that her daughter should be helpful there.

Amy, who was fond of Jessie, was delighted to think of having her company all the way to school, and her little fit of displeasure melted quite away. But when Florence was heard coming in, both girls were silent on their plans, knowing that she would only laugh at their wishing to do anything so dull.

17

CHAPTER III.

THE WORKING PARTY.

"Are these fruits of the sermon on Friday night?" said Miss Manners to Mr. Somers, as they finished winding up their parish accounts on Monday morning. "Not only, as you know, here is Grace Hollis wanting to join Mrs. Somers's Tuesday working parties, Jessie begging to help at the Sunday school; but I find that good little Amy Lee went and sat with poor Edwin Smithers for half an hour on Sunday after church, showing him pictures, and she has promised his mother to come and look in on him every day. It is very nice of the Lees to have thought of it, and to spare her."

"Yes," said Mrs. Somers, "the Lees are always anxious to do right."

"I had a talk with Charlotte just now. She came to get some flannel for Mrs. Long. She says she will make it up for her, if the old woman can have it out of the club. Well, she says it is quite striking how all those girls have been moved by Mr. Soulsby's sermon on Friday evening. Amy came home and nearly said it all off to her Aunt Rose, and the girls were all talking about it in the workroom in the morning, full of earnestness to make some effort."

"I saw they were looking very attentive," said Mr. Somers. "Shall you accept Jessie Hollis's help?"

"I think I can make a class up for her."

"I suppose it would be a pity to check her, but do you imagine that she knows anything?"

"I don't know; but she is not at all a stupid girl, and she cannot go far wrong with the questions on the Catechism and Gospels that I shall give her. Indeed I had thought of asking her and Margaret Roller, and, perhaps, Amy Lee, to come and prepare the lessons here on Friday evenings after church."

"A good plan," said Mr. Somers, "if it be not giving you too much to do."

"Not a bit, especially at this time of year, when nobody wants me in the evenings. My only doubt is whether it is not keeping the girls out too late, but I will see whether it can be managed. The children might be better taught, and the teachers might learn something themselves in this indirect way."

Perhaps this was Miss Dora's way of acting on the sermon, but she could not begin that week, as a friend was coming to spend the Friday with her.

Meantime Grace Hollis had joined the working party that met every

Tuesday afternoon for an hour to make clothes for a very poor district in London. She had been sometimes known to say that it was all waste of time to make things and send them away to thriftless, shiftless folk; but she had heard something of the love of our neighbour, and our membership with the rest of our Lord's Body, which had touched her heart. So she brought her thimble and needle, to join the working party who sat round the Rectory dining-table. Mrs. Somers and Miss Manners shook hands, made her welcome, and found her a seat and some work. Grace looked about her to be sure who the party were. Mrs. Nowell, the gardener's wife, sat next to her. Then came little Miss Agnes from the Hall, sewing hard away, and Lucy Drew from Chalk-pit Farm, who was about her age, next to her, and old Miss Pemberton knitting.

"A mixed lot," said Grace to herself, and then her eye lit upon deformed Naomi Norris, of whom she did not approve at all. Did not the girl come of a low dissenting family, and had not her father the presumption to keep a little shop in Hazel Lane which took away half the custom, especially as they pretended to make toffee? Meanwhile here was Miss Wenlock, the governess at the squire's, and Miss Dora reading aloud to the party in turn. It was the history of some mission work in London, and Miss Lee, who was there, listened with great pleasure, as did many of the others. Indeed she well might, for her eldest sister's son hoped one day to be a missionary. But Grace was not used to being read to, and, as she said, "it fidgeted her sadly," and she was wondering all the time what mistakes mother would make in the shop without her, and she began to be haunted with a doubt whether she had put out a parcel of raisins that Farmer Drew's man was to call for. The worry about it prevented her from attending to a word that was read; indeed she could hardly keep herself from jumping up, making up an excuse, and rushing home to see about the raisins!

Then she greatly disapproved of the shape of the bedgown she had been set to make, and did not believe it would sit properly. It was ladies' cutting towards which she felt contemptuous, and yet she would have thought it impolite to interfere. Besides, it might make the whole sitting go on longer, and Grace was burning to get home. At last the reading ended, but oh! my patience, that creature Naomi was actually putting herself forward to ask some nonsensical question, where some place was, and Miss Agnes must needs get a map, and every one go and look at it—Grace too, not to be behindhand or uncivil to the young ladies; but had not she had enough of maps and such useless stupid things long ago when she left school at Miss Perkins's?

When at last this was over, Mrs. Somers came and spoke to her while she was putting on her hat, and thanked her pleasantly, saying that she was afraid that beginning in the middle of a book made it less interesting, but that one day more would finish it. Then she added "I don't like the pattern of that bedgown, do you?"

"No, Mrs. Somers, not at all," replied Grace. "It quite went against me to put good work into it."

"I wonder whether you could help us to a better shape next time," said Mrs. Somers. "We should be very much obliged to you. This pattern came out of a needlework book, and I am not satisfied about it."

Grace promised, and went away in better humour, but more because she had been made important than because she cared for what she had been doing. She was glad no one could say she had been behindhand with her service, but it was a burthen to her, and she did not open her mind to enter into it so as to make it otherwise.

Indeed, her mind was more full of her accounts and the bad debts, and of the cheapest way of getting in her groceries than of anything else. As she walked back through the village she wondered whether Mrs. Somers and Miss Manners would send to her mother's for their brown sugar this summer. That would make it worth while to go to a better but more expensive place, and have in a larger stock; and Grace went on reckoning the risk all the time, and wondering whether the going to the working parties would secure the ladies' custom. In that case the time would not be wasted. It did not come into Grace's head whether what she had thought of for the service of God she might be turning to the service of Mammon, if she only just endured it for the sake of standing well with the gentry. But then, was it not her duty to consider her shop and her mother's interest?

She was quite vexed and angry when she saw Jessie go and fetch the big Family Bible that evening, turning off the whole pile of lesson-books to which it formed the base.

"Now what can you be doing that for?" she said sharply.

"I want to prepare my lesson for to-morrow," said Jessie.

"And is not a little Bible good enough for you, without upsetting the whole table?"

"My Bible has got no references," said Jessie.

"And what do little children like that want of references? If you are to be turning the house upside down and wasting time like that over preparing as you call it, I don't know as ma will let you undertake it."

"I have ironed all the collars and cuffs, Grace," said Jessie; "yes, and looked over the stockings."

Grace had no more to say; she knew Jessie had wonderful eyes for a ladder or a hole; but it worried her and gave her a sense of disrespect that the pyramid which surmounted the big Bible should be interfered with, or that the Book itself should have its repose interfered with "for a pack of dirty children," when it had never been opened before except to register christenings, or to be spread out and read when some near relation died, as part of the mourning ceremony.

It really made her feel as if something unfortunate had happened to see the large print pages on the little round table, and her sister peering into the references and looking them out in her own little Bible, then diligently marking them.

Her mother, too, asked what Jessie was about, and though she did not say anything against her employment, their looking on, and the expression on Grace's face, worried Jessie so much that she could not think, and only put a slip of paper into her own book at each she found. The chapter she had chosen was the Parable of the Sower, on which she had once heard a sermon. She was amazed to find how many parallel passages there were, and how beautifully they explained one another when she made time for comparing them on Sunday morning. She saw herself beforehand expounding them to the children, and winning their hearts, as her friend in the hospital had described, and she was quite ready in her neat black silk and fur jacket, with a little blue velvet hat, when Amy Lee came to call for her, in her grey merino, black cloth coat, and little hat to match.

They met Miss Manners at the school door, and were pleasantly greeted, and taken into the large cheerful room, all hung round with maps and pictures, where the classes were assembling, and one or two of the other teachers had come.

The bell was heard ringing, and while the children trooped in, Miss Manners showed Jessie a chair with some books laid open upon it, the class register on the top, and said:

"I am sorry there has not been time to talk over your work this week; but I have laid out the books for you, and if you are in any difficulty come and ask me."

By this time the children had come in and taken their places, and Jessie was pleased to see that her class was of children of eight or nine years old— not such little ones as Amy had threatened her with. Miss Manners went to the harmonium and gave out a Sunday morning hymn, which was very sweetly sung, and then she read prayers, everybody kneeling, and making the responses, so that Jessie enjoyed it greatly, and felt quite refreshed by the prayer for a blessing on the teachers and the taught. Then Miss Manners told the eight little girls who stood in a row that Miss Hollis would teach them, and she hoped they would be very good and steady and obedient, and say their lessons perfectly.

Jessie knew all but two who came from the other end of the parish, and were not customers of her mother—at least she knew what families they belonged to, and had only to learn their Christian names from her list.

"Collect, please teacher," said the first girl, Susan Bray, very much in the voice in which she would have said "Candles, please miss," in the shop.

The Prayer-book was uppermost, and Jessie found she had to hear the Collect for the day repeated by five perfectly, by two rather badly, and one broke down altogether. The question-book lay open under it. Some of the questions were very easy, but of others Jessie was not sure that the children were right when they replied to some quite glibly, and she was not sure how to help them in others.

Then followed the opening of books again. Jessie was longing to give out all she had to say about the Sower, and began bidding them turn to it in St. Matthew, but Susan Bray stopped her most decisively. "Oh! please teacher, we've done that ever so long ago. We always reads the Gospel for the day, and here's the question-book, and it's got answers." And she thrust it right under the nose of Jessie, who by this time did not quite love Miss Susan Bray. She had plainly been sharp enough to see when her teacher was at fault.

The children read the Gospel for the day. It was Refreshing Sunday, so it was not a difficult one; the children were ready with the answers till the application came, and then Jessie had again to help them, which she did by reading the printed answers and making them repeat them after her, word for word. While she was doing this with Mary Smithers, who certainly was dulness itself, at one end of the class, there was a whispering at the other, and she saw two children trying on each other's gloves, and she quickly put an end to that, and went on with another question and answer. The moment her eye was off Susan Bray and Lily Bell, however, they began comparing some gay cards. Jessie turned on them: "You are playing with those things. Give them to me."

Lily Bell began to cry, and Susan pertly said, "It's our markers, teacher."

"I don't care. I won't have you idle. Give them to me, this instant."

Just then the church bell began to ring, and there was a general moving; but Jessie would not be beaten, and caused the two cards to be given up to her. The girls both cried with all their might while she was marking the class down, and, as they no doubt intended, Miss Manners came to see what was the matter.

"Please, ma'am, teacher has taken away our markers, and we shan't know where our Psalms is."

"They were playing with them," said Jessie.

"We wasn't. We was finding our Psalms," said Susan.

"You should not have done so while Miss Hollis was teaching," said Miss Manners. "I hope, if she is good enough to give them back to you, that you will attend better in the afternoon."

Jessie felt it all a little flat and disappointing, all the more so that Amy Lee joined her, and talked all the way to church about the children, who had all passed through her hands when she was a pupil teacher, telling all their little tiresome ways. It seemed to rub off all the gloss, and to change her scheme of feeding the young lambs for the Great Shepherd's sake into a mere struggle with tiresome, fidgety children.

Still her hopes and her spirits rose again at church. She had her expounding of the Sower on her mind, and hoped yet to deliver it when she went to afternoon school; but there proved to be the Catechism and a whole set of hymns to be said, and questions to be asked about them. These questions did not come very readily to such an unpractised tongue as hers, and she thought she could lead off into the discourse she had thought out over the Bible. But she had hardly gone through twenty words before she saw a squabble going on between Lily Bell and Mary Smithers, and she had no sooner separated them, and taken up the thread of her discourse about grace being sown and watered in our hearts, than Susan Bray popped up up with "Please, teacher, it's time to read to us—Its *Miss Angelina*," pointing to a little gay story-book.

"You should not be rude, and interrupt," said Jessie; whereupon Susan pouted, the two idlest began to play with each other's fingers, and, as soon as she paused to take breath, Lily Bell jumped up, and brought her the book open.

She had to give up the point, and begin to read something that did not seem to her nearly so improving as her own discourse, as it was all about a doll left behind upon a heath; but the children listened to it eagerly.

Was this all the good she was to do by sacrificing all her time on Sunday? Like Grace, she felt much inclined to give it up, and all the more when Florence Cray came into the work-room the next morning, laughing and saying—

"Well, the impudence of some folk! There was that there little Bray! I hear that she should say that Miss Hollis was put to teach her, and she warn't agoing to care for one as wasn't a lady."

"I can make her mind me fast enough," said Amy.

"O, you are bred to be a teacher," said Florence; "that doesn't count. Nobody else should trouble themselves with the tiresome little ungrateful things. I'm sure I wouldn't; but then I don't set up for goodness, nor want to be thought better than other folk."

Jessie had known that something of this kind would be said, and was prepared for it; but the child's speech vexed her sorely. However, she said—

"I'm not going to be beat by a chit like that," and at that moment Miss Lee came in, and that kind of chatter ceased.

But Jessie's cheeks burned over her work, and she thought how foolish she had been to let her fancy for doing good, and trying to live up to the sermon, lead her where she was allowed to do nothing, but get herself teased and insulted, right and left.

Should she give up? That would look so silly. Yes, but would it not serve Miss Manners right for giving her such stupid, unspiritual kind of teaching to do, and also serve the children right for their pertness and ingratitude?

No, she could not give up in this way. She had begun, and she must go on, at least till she had some reason for giving up respectably and civilly—only she wished she had known how unlike it was to what she had expected before she had undertaken it!

Then she was sensible of a certain odd, uppish, self-asserting feeling within her. She used to have it in old times, but she had learnt to distrust it, and to know that it generally came when she was in a bad way.

Was she thinking of pleasing herself, or of offering a little work to please God, and try to let the good seed turn to good fruit? Ah! but was it all a mistake? Was becoming a mark for Susan Bray to worry, doing any good at all?

CHAPTER IV.

TEACHER AMY.

I⊤ was a pleasant sight for Amy when poor little Edwin Smithers's pale face brightened up, as she opened his door.

He was not like the rough little monkey she had known at the infant school, who had only seemed to want to learn as little, and to play as many tricks, as he could. In the hospital, the attention kind people had paid him had quickened up his understanding, and mended his manners. He had been petted and amused there, and the being left alone in the dull cottage was a sad trial to him. His mother had regular work, and so had her elder brother, but this kept them out all day from eight till five, except that Mrs. Smithers kept Friday to do her own washing in. She was obliged to be away even at dinner time, as her work lay far from home, and she gave her next-door neighbour, Mrs. Rowe, a shilling a week to keep up the fire, look in on the sick boy, and give him his dinner.

She was unlucky in her neighbour. Many women would have gladly given far more kind service for no pay at all, but they were too far off, and Mrs. Rowe made it a rule to "do nothing for nothing."

His brother and sisters came in for a little while at twelve, their dinner time, but they wanted to go out to play, and had no notion of amusing him; indeed he was glad when they went away; Charlie clumped about so, and made such a noise, and little Jenny would take away his picture books or the toys that had been given him in the hospital.

Then Polly would call her a naughty girl, and snatch them from her, and so his little wooden horse lost its head, and his railway train was uncoupled, and one wheel pulled off; and when old Mrs. Rowe found him crying, all she said was, "Dear! dear! don't ye fret now, don't ye!" and when that did not make him stop crying, she said he was a bad boy to make such a work about nothing. When she was a girl, nobody had frail trade like that, all painted and gaudy, to play with; a bit of an oyster-shell or a crab's claw was enow for them. He had got into such a caddle as never was too!

So she began to shake up his couch, not in the least guessing how she was hurting and jarring his poor hip; and when he cried out and tried to drive her away, she thought it was all naughtiness, and declared that he was such a bad boy that she should go away and leave him to himself.

The Lees dined at one, and work did not begin till two; so Amy had a good half-hour to spend on the little boy before she was wanted again.

"Going to see Ted, be ye?" said Mrs. Rowe, as she stood at her door, while Amy opened the wicket. "A proper fractious little to-äd he be, upon my word an' honour! They do spile children in them hospitals, so as one can't do nothing with 'em."

Amy looked at Mrs. Rowe, a very clean woman, but with a face and fists that looked as if they had been cut out of the toughest part of an old pollard ash, and a mouth that shut up like the snap of a gin. "Poor little fellow!" said Amy, and in she went.

She was on her knees at once by the poor little boy, coaxing him and comforting him, and feeding him with some of the stew that Aunt Charlotte had kept warm for him. Then he told how Polly had taken away his horse and his train and broken them. Amy looked about, and presently found the wheel. A little hooking together was all the repair the train wanted, and Edwin was soon happy with it; while, as to the horse, he was past Amy's present mending, but she would take it home, and next time father had out the glue- pot she would put on the head.

Then Amy brought out a little book with the early Bible history in pictures. She showed Edwin one every day when she came, and told him about it whenever he did not know the story before, or helped him to enter a little more into it. She was surprised sometimes to find that he had carried notions away from school even when she had thought him only dull and giddy. Then he was pleased to say over the hymns he had learnt in the infant school, and to talk a little about it. Amy was quite surprised to find how his mind had grown since he had been ill, and how pleased he was to be taught a little verse of prayer to say when he was in pain.

She made him quite comfortable, filled up his mug of water, which the other children had upset, put some primroses in a cup where he could look at them, wrote a copy on his slate, and ruled some lines, caught the cat and put her before him, found the place in his easy story-book, and left him with a kiss, promising to come again to-morrow.

It was very pleasant to be the bright spot in that poor little life; and Amy that afternoon stitched into little Miss Hilda's tucks, to the whirr of her machine, a whole pensive castle in the air about the dear little fellow who was not long for this world, and whose pillow was cheered and his soul trained for Paradise by his dear teacher, who came day by day to lead him in the path to Heaven. The tears came into her eyes at the thought of how beautiful and touching it would all be—how she would lay a wreath of white roses on his coffin, and——

"What are you winking about, Amy? Go nearer the window if you want more light," said Aunt Rose, in a brisk, business-like voice, not at all like her dreams.

Amy was glad to move, feeling a little ashamed of being detected in crying beforehand about her own good works; and as she approached the window, she looked out over the lemon-plant and exclaimed—"There's Miss Manners!"

Miss Manners was really coming into the shop, and her little Skye terrier was already running on into the work-room, for he was great friends with Amy; he sniffed about, sat up, and gave his paw, and let her show off his tricks while his mistress was talking to Aunt Charlotte.

Then she came on, nodded kindly a little greeting to each as they all rose, and said that she had been thinking that it would be a good thing for all the teachers to meet for half an hour before evensong on Fridays and look over their Sunday work together, so as to make it chime together. She said she found it was done at Ellerby, and was very helpful to all; and perhaps, when he had time, Mr. Somers would come in and help them. If they looked over the subjects beforehand, they could note the difficulties, and then she could refer to books, or ask Mr. Somers.

Amy and Jessie both uttered some thanks, and Aunt Rose observed that it was very kind in Miss Dora, and that it would be very nice for the girls. Florence did not speak, but they saw her face and the gesture of her foot, and when Miss Lee walked out with the lady through the garden, Florence broke out—

"Well, how fond some folks are of being put to school, to be sure!"

"'Tisn't school," said Amy, "it is reading with Miss Manners in her drawing-room."

"O yes; she makes you think yourselves ladies just to keep on grinding you at the teaching for ever; but I likes my fun when my work's done. I don't wonder at Amy Lee—she knows nothing better than sitting poked up and prim in Miss Manners's room; but for you, Jessie Hollis, who have seen a bit of the world, I should have thought you'd have more spirit than not even to be let to teach half a dozen dirty children without having your instructions."

Here Miss Lee returned, and Florence applied herself to tacking in the lining again, while Jessie muttered to herself, "If I'm to teach them at all, I'd rather do it properly."

Jessie really wished it. Perhaps the notion of seeing the inside of Miss Manners's drawing-room made it doubly pleasant, for Jessie had eyes that really could not help taking note of everything, though there was no harm in that when she kept them in due control. She had been in the dining-room before, and she hoped much that the class would be in the other room, though she was half ashamed of caring.

Grace came home better satisfied on Tuesday, because her patterns had been much appreciated, though she still said the reading worrited her, and Naomi Norris gave herself airs.

Jessie and Amy, however, went together on Friday, and found Margaret Roller, the pupil teacher, and Miss Pemberton, an elderly farmer's daughter, who always taught the little ones on Sunday, were ready there, and in the drawing-room.

How pretty it was, with fresh delicate soft pink and white cretonne covers, and curtains worked with—was it really a series of old nursery tales? And coloured tiles, with Æsop's fables round the fireplace, pictures, books, and pretty things that all looked as if they had a history. Jessie's bright eyes took note of all in a flash, and then she tried to command them. Miss Manners gave them all their greeting, settled them all comfortably, and then began by reading to them a short paper in a little book upon the spirit of the whole Sunday, asking them in turn to look out and read the texts referred to, which Margaret and Amy did with a rapidity that astonished Jessie.

Once she lost the thread in wondering what was looking out of a half-opened basket; but she caught herself up, and found that there was infinitely more connection and meaning in the passages appointed for the Sunday than she had ever guessed.

Then Miss Manners asked whether they had any questions to ask; Margaret had one or two, which sounded very hard to Jessie, and she would never have thought of. It was the Fifth Sunday in Lent for which they were preparing, and they were respecting the unusually long and difficult Gospel for the day. Margaret wanted to know whether the words "By whom do your sons cast them out?" really meant that devils were actually cast out by the Jews. Miss Manners thought they were, and she looked out, and showed Margaret, a very curious account of the seal and sacred words of exorcism which were supposed to come from Solomon; but she advised the teachers not to dwell much on this branch of the subject, but to draw out most the portion about the strong man armed, and the warning against the return of Satan to the soul whence he had been once driven out.

Then Jessie observed that she had not thought such things happened in these days, and Miss Manners had to explain to her how the possession then permitted was here treated as an allegory to all times, of the evil once cast off returning again if not resolutely excluded by prayer and a strong purpose blessed by the grace of God.

It soon became plain to Jessie that she was ignorant of much which the others knew quite well, and when the Church bell began to chime, and all rose to go, she obtained a moment in which to say, with something like a tear in her eye—

"Indeed, Miss Manners, I ought not to have undertaken it. I see I am not fit to teach."

"I do not think you can tell without a longer trial," was the answer, kindly given.

"But I am so ignorant!" said Jessie. "There is so much in these things that I never thought of, and the others seem to know all about it."

"It has been their regular Sunday school round for years," said Miss Manners, "so it would be strange if they did not. But perhaps you will do all the better for coming to it fresh; and I am sure you are willing to take pains and prepare."

"Yes," said Jessie, slowly, "if——You'll excuse me, Miss Manners, but ——"

"Please say it, Jessie," said the lady; "or shall I say it for you? This asking idle children very simple questions does not seem to you to be spiritual enough to be doing much good?"

"Yes, ma'am, if you will excuse me. I thought there was to be more expounding of Scripture."

"We must do what we can to get the children to attend to," said Miss Manners. "Even if we could get them to sit still while we expounded, I am afraid they would not attend or take in what we said. Nothing is of use with such young things but keeping them on the alert with questions, and trying to keep up their attention by being alive with them ourselves. We must try to put into them the sense of God's love to them, of their own duty, and so on; but rather by the tone of our questions about the lessons they learn than by discoursing long to them. You can only fill a little narrow-mouthed pitcher with a few drops at a time put right in. If you pour a great stream over it, most will splash over, and very little go in. I am afraid the children were tiresome last Sunday. It is their nature always to try their strength with a new teacher; but if you are firm and gentle, and show them that you *will* be minded, and keep them interested, they will soon be manageable. Then, Jessie, there is good hope that you may be sowing good seed, though you and I may not always see the fruit here, and it is nearly sure to be long before we can even trace the green blade."

CHAPTER V.

THE TROUSSEAU.

Miss Manners's words stayed with Jessie. She had plenty of sense and spirit, as well as a real wish to do right, and a yearning to spread the great Light round her. To be sure, the going to some mission in a dreadfully ignorant and wicked place would have seemed more like a good work than just taking a class who would be taught and cared for even without her help.

But she could see that if she could not keep these tidy little trained children in order, she would not have much chance with the street Arabs she had read of.

She got on much better the next Sunday. She kept the children interested almost all the time, all except the two lowest, who were determined to chatter till she made one stand on each side of her, and then one of them, Emma Lott, chose to howl till Miss Manners came to see what was the matter; but she did not get much by that, for she was only told that she was very naughty not to mind Miss Hollis, and desired to stop crying directly, which she did; and then Miss Manners asked Miss Hollis to be so kind as not to take away her ticket, if she would try to behave well for the rest of the day.

Once more Lily Bell was so kind as to inform "teacher" that Susan said "she didn't care, not for she." To which Jessie coolly answered that she hoped Susan would soon learn to care for being a good girl, taking care not to look the least mortified, so that the information fell very flat. After that she had no more trouble with sauciness from the children; she began to find that Susan was clever and bright, and that Kate May and Lucy Elwood were very nice little maidens, who seemed to care to be good. They brought her flowers, told her funny little bits of news about baby beginning to walk, and mother going to Ellerby, and she found the time spent at school a very pleasant part of her Sunday; while as to the hours of preparation with Miss Manners, she enjoyed them so much that it was quite a blank if that lady had any engagement to prevent her from receiving her little party of teachers.

Jessie found herself learning much more than she taught. Her quick nature could not but look into everything thoroughly, and when she had been once shown how to throw all her mind as well as her soul into the study of the Bible and Prayer-book, she found ever new delight in them. She began to find it helped her to pray with her understanding, as well as with her spirit at Church; to care more for her prayers at home, and to feel more on the times of the Holy Communion. She made her last year's hat serve again with a fresh tulle trimming, that she might buy herself a "Teacher's Bible," and not worry her mother and Grace any more by disturbing the big one, since they thought it honouring such a Bible to let it alone.

Mrs. Hollis did read the Psalms and one Lesson every day. She said she had once promised Amy Lee, aunt to the present Amy, and she had hardly ever missed doing so.

But Grace had not time. Just after Whitsuntide the daughter of a very rich farmer in the neighbourhood was engaged to be married, and wanted a quantity of fine work to be done for her, making underlinen and embroidering marks to handkerchiefs.

She came with her mother to offer the work to Miss Lee, giving six weeks for it, but it was more than Aunt Rose thought right to undertake in the time. She said she could not get it done without disappointing several persons, and that she was very sorry, but that she could only undertake two sets of the things in the time.

Mrs. Robson, the mother, was vexed and half angry. She said she hated common shop-work, and ready-made things, and she had taken a fancy to what she had seen of Miss Lee's work. She even offered to increase the payment, but Rose Lee stood firm. She said there was no one at hand whom she could hire and entrust with such work, and that she could not feel it right to undertake it, as it would only lead to breaking her engagements.

"O, very well; I see you don't care to oblige me," said the lady, twirling off with her very tight skirts, and whisking up a train like a fish's tail. "No, I will not break the set. I am not accustomed to refusals."

And off the two ladies drove, and Jessie told the story at home with a great deal of spirit.

"Now that's just like Rose Lee," said Grace. "She won't make a bit of exertion for her own good!"

"Well," said Jessie, "you know we should have to work awfully hard if she took it in hand."

"I suppose she would have paid you for extra hours," said Grace sharply.

"Miss Rose said it was the way to ruin a girl's health to set her to do such a lot of work," said Jessie.

"And quite right too," put in her mother. "I knew a girl who was apprenticed to a dressmaker, and sat up five nights when they had two black jobs one after the other, and that girl's eyes never was the same again!"

"Besides," added Jessie, "there's so much in hand."

"Well, it might not do to offend Mrs. or Miss Manners, but—"

"O, it is not that! The children's things were sent home yesterday. I wish you could have seen them, they were loves; and Miss Manners has got a new dress from London. She let Miss Lee see it, and take the pattern of the trimming. No, but Mrs. Drew has sent her Swiss cambric to be made up for Miss Alice, and Miss Pemberton has a new carmelite to be finished, and there are some dresses for the maids at the hall, all promised by Midsummer day."

"Pooh! Customers like that can wait."

"I don't see that it is a bit more right to disappoint them than any one else," said Jessie sturdily.

"Old Miss Pemberton, to be compared with a lady like that!" exclaimed Grace.

"It doesn't make much odds as to right or wrong," said Jessie, "but I don't think Mrs. Robson is much of a lady, to judge by the way she gave her orders and flounced off in a huff."

"A lady," said Mrs. Hollis, contemptuously, "I should think not. Why, her father kept the 'White Feathers' at Ellerby; and Robson, he rose up just by speculations, as they call them; but I've seen him a little greengrocer's errand-boy, with a face like a dirty potato."

"They can pay, any way," said Grace. "Folks say Robson could buy out our squire, ay, and my lord himself, if he chose."

"And I'm sure," said Jessie, "she and her daughter had clothes on that must cost forty or fifty pounds apiece. Such a fur cloak, lined with ermine; and the young lady's jacket was sealskin, trimmed ever so deep with sable, and a hummingbird in her hat. They say little Miss Hilda saw her and cried for pity of the poor dear little bird."

"Well, I'll tell you what," said Grace, "I'll set off this minute to Newcome Park, and see if I can't get the work, or at least some of it. You and I can do plain work as well any day as Rose Lee, Jessie."

"Yes," said Jessie, "but I have my time at Miss Lee's all the same."

"Of course, child; but there are the evenings, and I can sit to it while mother minds the shop."

"Don't undertake more than you can manage, Grace," said Mrs. Hollis.

"Trust me for that, mother. You can wash up, Jessie; I can get there before they go to dress for dinner. It is a capital thing! It will just make up for that bad debt of Long's, and help us to get in a real genteel stock of summer goods."

Grace managed the house, and her mother, who durst not say a word when she was set on a thing; and as to Jessie, her sister always treated her as a rather naughty, idle child.

The girl had struggled hotly against this, but it had always ended in getting into such a temper, and saying such fierce and violent things, that she had been much grieved and ashamed of herself, and now felt it better to let Grace have her way than to get into a dispute which was sure to make her do wrong.

But when Grace, as neat as a new pin, had tripped out of the house, Mrs. Hollis and Jessie looked at one another, as if they had a pretty severe task set them.

"Well, I think we could have managed without," said Mrs. Hollis, "but to be sure it is as well to be on the safe side; though I'd rather be without the money than be at all the trouble and hurry this work will be!"

"I am sure I had," said Jessie. "I wish I had said nothing about it. Grace can't bear to hear of anything going that she has not got."

"Any way," said Mrs. Hollis, "you shall not be put upon, Jessie, after all your work at Miss Lee's. You shall not be made to sit at your needle all the evening. It is not good for your health, and so I shall tell Grace."

Jessie thanked her mother, but had little hope that she would be able to hold out against one so determined as her sister. Neither mother nor daughter would have broken her heart if Grace's application had come too late, but no such thing! It had been dark about an hour when she was driven up to the door in a dog-cart, out of which huge rolls of linen were lifted, enough, as it seemed, to stock the shop. Grace shook hands with the smart groom who had driven her, thanked him, and came in in high spirits.

Mrs. Robson had been most gracious! She said she had feared being obliged to put up with mere warehouse work, and that she could not bear; but country people were so lazy and disobliging. It was not what she was used to.

Grace had been taken up into the young lady's own room, and oh! what she had to tell about tall cheval glasses, and ivory-backed brushes, and rose-coloured curtains, and marble-topped washhand-stands, and a bed and wardrobe of inlaid wood, with beautiful birds and flowers, and gold-topped bottles and boxes, and downy chairs! The description was enough to last a week, and indeed it did, for fresh details came out continually. It almost made Jessie jealous for Miss Manners. Once when she had been caught in a sudden shower and arrived wet through she had been taken up to Miss Manners's bed-room to take off her boots and put on slippers.

And there was only a plain little iron bed, uncurtained, and the floor was bare except for rugs at the hearth and bed-side, and the furniture was nothing but white dimity. The chimney ornaments and the washhand-stand looked like those in a nursery—as indeed they well might, for they had belonged to Miss Dora nearly all her life; they all had stories belonging to them, were keepsakes from dear friends, and she would not have given one, no, not the shell cat with an ear off, nor the little picture made of coloured sand, for Miss Robson's finest gilded box, unless indeed that had come in the same way.

And there were two prints on the walls, very grave and beautiful, which made one feel like being in Church, and so did the illuminated texts, though all were not equally well done, some being painted by her little nieces. Jessie had a feeling in her mind that there was something finer and nobler in not making one's own nest so very splendid and luxurious, but she knew Grace would laugh at the notion, so she said nothing of the difference, while her mother said, "Dear, dear!" and "Think of that!" at each new bit of magnificence she heard of.

Grace had her patterns and materials, and the fineness of them, and beauty of the lace provided for the trimming, were quite delightful to look at.

The payment was to be very handsome, and Grace felt secure of carrying through the work in time, with the help of her mother and sister.

"You shall have your share, Jessie," she said. "See, here are some sweet French cambric handkerchiefs to be marked in embroidery. 'I have a sister who can embroider beautifully,' says I, and they just jumped at it. 'Nina' is the name to be worked in the corners."

"Oh, I like embroidery," cried Jessie. "Thank you, Grace."

"There's six dozen," said Grace, "and you'll be able to do one a day. Four pence a letter. Why it will be quite a little fortune to you," said Grace, overpowered with her own generosity; and Jessie on her side thought of the many things 4*l.* 16*s.* would do for her.

CHAPTER VI.

STITCH, STITCH, STITCH.

It must be confessed that Mrs. Hollis and Jessie had a hard time of it while those wedding clothes were being made!

There was no time for anything, certainly not for cooking. They ate the cold Sunday joint as long as it lasted, and lived the rest of the week on bread and cheese, and Australian meat now and then.

Grace got up before four every morning, and there was not much peace in bed for any one after that.

Of course the shop had to be minded, and that Mrs. Hollis did, but she was expected to be at her needle at every spare moment; and for the needful cleaning and rougher work, Grace got a woman for a couple of hours who came cheap, because she did not bear a very good character. Mrs. Hollis did not much like having her about, but, as Grace said, one or other of them always had an eye upon her, and she was only there for a couple of hours in the morning.

It was lucky kettles could boil themselves, or there might not even have been tea, and as to going to Mrs. Somers's working parties, Grace declared it to be impossible.

"I've got something else to do," she said, decidedly. "The lady can't expect me to stand in my own light."

And when she saw Jessie on Friday evening put away her work and fetch her hat and books, she cried out against such idling, and said it must be given up.

"No," said Jessie. "I can't give up my Church and my preparation with Miss Manners."

"Nonsense! You see I've given up my working party."

"Yes; but I can't give up mine," said Jessie. "Oh, Grace, we thought so much about trying to do what we could."

"And so I am!" said Grace. "No one can say I am not doing my duty to my family, and that's better than throwing away my time on a lot of beggarly folk that don't deserve nothing. And you ought to know better, Jessie."

"I must have my lesson prepared," said she in return.

"As if you couldn't teach that there Bell girl without going to read with Miss Manners first! You'll never have those handkerchiefs done!"

"I did two letters extra this morning," said Jessie.

"Ah, that's very fine, but if you get one of your headaches——"

The sound of that word alarmed Mrs. Hollis. Jessie had had a bad illness about a year ago, and the mother could not part with her anxiety about her. In she came, with the tea-cup she was washing in her hand.

"Has Jessie got a headache?" she inquired.

"Oh no, mother, thank you. Grace is only putting a case."

"Yes; I am asking her what she thinks will become of the work if she is to go and take her pleasure whenever she likes. She talks of working extra; but supposing she had a headache, she'd be sorry she had thrown away her time."

"Dear, dear," said Mrs. Hollis; "'tis the very way to make her have a headache to keep her poor nose to the grindstone. The doctor, he says to me, 'She've had a shock, and she'll require care, and not to be overstrained.' And I tell you, Grace, I won't have Jessie put upon, and kept muzzing over her needle like a blackamoor slave, without a taste of fresh air. So run away, Jessie, and get your walk."

"Thank you, mother."

And Jessie, who did not feel bound to obey her sister, ran lightly off, hoping poor mother would not be very fiercely talked at by Grace. She herself was clear that work undertaken for God's sake should not be dropped when one's own gain began to clash with it; while Grace, who had always been held up as the model, helpful good daughter, plainly thought, "working for one's family," and securing something extra, was such a reason as to make it a sort of duty to throw over all she had taken up under the spur of that sermon in the spring. Jessie had no headache, but she was weary, vexed, and teased, and

> "Stitch, stitch, stitch,
> Seam and gusset and band,"

rang in her ears, so that she specially felt rested and soothed by the calm and quiet of Miss Manners's pretty room, with the open windows and the scent of flowers coming in from the garden.

The subject was next Sunday's Gospel, about the Great Supper and the excuse-making guests. Miss Manners read out part of Archbishop Trench's comment on the Parable before she talked to the teachers about what they were to say to their classes; and Jessie felt deeply that to let herself be engrossed by this undertaking, so as to allow no time for her religious duties, would be only too like the guests who went "one to his farm, and another to his merchandise." She was advised to make it a lesson to her class against false or insufficient excuses, such as saying they were late at school because mother wanted them to take a message, when they had dawdled all the way instead of hastening to school. Miss Manners lent the volume of Miss Edgeworth's *Rosamond* to Jessie, to read the chapter on Excuses to her girls, so as to bring home the lesson, though she was to carry it higher, and put them in mind that if they put their duties aside for these little things now, they would be learning to forget their Heavenly Master for earthly matters, and would never taste of His supper.

It made Jessie doubly and trebly determined that she would not take a lie-a-bed on Sunday morning to make up for loss of rest before, and thus miss the early Celebration on her monthly Sunday. Indeed, she felt drawn to come oftener, if it would not be presuming.

She came home from Church in the summer twilight, when even Grace could not work, and was standing a moment at the door before lighting the lamp.

"Well, miss, I hope you have wasted enough daylight," she said.

"I hope it wasn't quite wasted," said Jessie, cheerfully. "I shall work ever so much quicker for the rest I have had."

And she was as good as her word, and spent an hour in her pleasant embroidery of the pretty white letters of the name which she really delighted in doing, only she would have liked a fresh pattern instead of making all the seventy-two Ninas exactly alike.

She was at work before half-past six the next day, and had three more letters done before it was time to go to Miss Lee's, where it was a busy day of finishing work; and when at three o'clock the last stitch was put to the dress that had been made out of Mrs. Drew's cambric, Miss Lee asked Jessie to carry it home, suspecting that the walk would be good for her.

It was rather hot, but Jessie did enjoy the lanes, with their flowery banks, and the sweet smells of the hay, and she felt much brightened and refreshed. When she came near the house, she saw some one sitting in a basket-chair in the porch, and knew that it was Miss Needwood, a poor, sickly orphan relation of Mrs. Drew's, who was always trying situations as nursery governess, or reader, or the like, and leaving them because her health would not serve; and then she had no home to go to but Chalk-pit Farm. She was not so much above the Hollises as the farmer's own family, and was always friendly with them. She came to meet Jessie, shook hands with her, and explained that Mrs. Drew had been summoned to speak about some poultry, but would return in a moment if Miss Hollis would sit down.

"Are you stopping here for long?" asked Jessie.

"I don't know," said the poor girl, sadly; "I hoped I was settled in a nice situation; but my asthma was bad there, and the lady found it out, and it made her nervous, so here I am again. Mr. Drew, he is kind, and says I may make myself useful with teaching the children; but oh, dear! I don't know enough for that."

"I thought you had gone out for a nursery governess."

"Yes"—the tears came in her eyes;—"but I'll never try again. The elder young ladies made game of my French, and said I didn't spell as well as the little nursery girl. And it was true, Miss Hollis. I tried being a sewing-maid last, though Mrs. Drew didn't want folk to know it; but, you see, I hadn't health for that. They are very good here, and will keep me; but I am nothing but a burthen. If I could but hear of something to do—if only to keep me in clothes. I can do fancy-work, if I could get any."

"Can you embroider?" asked Jessie.

Miss Needwood took out her pocket-handkerchief, where her initials, H. N., were beautifully worked. Jessie had admired her own work, but this was much better. It was just such an N as she wanted, and she exclaimed—

"If you would be so kind as to lend me one of those for a pattern, I should be so much obliged."

"Do you embroider?" asked Miss Needwood. "I wish you could tell me if there is any shop at Ellerby or Carchester that would employ me; I should be so much happier."

Here Mrs. Drew came back, and looked over the dress which was to be sent to her daughter at her boarding-school, and thanked Jessie, and gave her the money for Miss Lee.

Miss Needwood had fetched the handkerchief, and Jessie took leave and walked home, thinking over what shops might possibly employ the poor girl. What a pity she had not those handkerchiefs to do, and why should she not do some of them?

Oh, Grace would never consent. Besides, Jessie had spent her 4*l.* 16*s.* in fancy already on the Offertory, savings bank, a present for mother, a pair of spectacles for old Dame Wall, a pretty new dress and hat for herself. Oh no, she must work on; it was such pretty work, and Grace would scorn her so if she gave up any part of it.

Jessie came home to find Mrs. Hollis in all the hard work and worry of a

Saturday evening, alone in the shop, with people waiting and getting cross. She had to hasten behind the counter and help as fast as she could. It was well that the Lees had given her a cup of tea when she brought in the money, for there was no quiet for more than an hour, and then the fire was found to have gone out while Grace was putting in gathers. Moreover, Jessie saw, with dismay, that the beefsteak-pie, which was to serve for the morrow, was not even made.

"Oh, I'll do that to-morrow morning," said Grace.

And when Jessie proceeded to tack in her clean collar and cuffs, Grace called out, raising her hot face from her work, that they might be pinned in on Sunday morning; it was only waste of time to do so now.

"I don't think that is using Sunday quite well," said Jessie.

"Well, I never heard there was any harm in sticking in a pin of a Sunday! Come, sit down, do, and don't keep fiddling about. You'll be behind with those handkerchiefs. Here, mother, you can finish this seam before dark."

"The place is in such a caddle," said poor Mrs. Hollis, looking ruefully round at her kitchen, which certainly did not wear at all its usual Saturday evening's aspect. "That Jenny Simkins, she do so stabble in and out, she only wants some one to clean after her."

"Oh, well, I'll see to that," said Grace, "when it gets too dark for work. One must put up with a little for such a chance as this."

Jessie felt that her poor mother was putting up with more than a little, as she saw her sit down with a sigh and try to thread her needle by the window. Jessie went across and did it for her, and put back the muslin blind so as to let in more light; then sat down to finish the "na" of her sixth Nina, rather wearily, and with an uncomfortable thought that Miss Needwood's satin-stitch looked better than her own.

Little "n" was done before the twilight tidying, which did not amount to much, for Grace soon lighted the lamp; but Jessie, in putting up the shop shutters, made the arm, which had once been crushed, tremble so much that she could not work without pricking her finger, and Mrs. Hollis really could not see. So Grace let them both go to bed, and Jessie half waked to hear her bustling about, and coming up herself just after the clock struck twelve. She would not have set a stitch on any account after that!

Jessie was up early enough to light the fire, and set out the breakfast things, and put on the kettle, while both her mother and Grace were still in bed. She had a peaceful, happy time then, but otherwise she had never known such an uncomfortable Sunday.

Mrs. Hollis was down when she came back, but was fretting over the very large bit that had gone out of the cheese. Jessie thought they had eaten it for want of meat; her mother suspected Jenny Simkins. Then she had not been allowed time to copy out her accounts into the book, and there had been a great puzzle between a three and a five on the slate last night, which seemed to have been worrying her all night in her dreams; and the uncleaned look of the house vexed her. She was tired and not like herself, and Jessie only left her for school and church on hearing Grace's step on the stairs.

At school she could forget all about it in the interest of teaching, but the worry returned when her mother's place was empty at the beginning of the service; and when Mrs. Hollis did come posting in at the end of the *Venite*, she was so hot and panting that she had to sit down and fan herself with her pocket-handkerchief all through the Psalms, and Jessie even feared she might be going to faint.

"Oh dear," Mrs. Hollis mourned, when they came out of church, "she had never been so upset before, but she had been so put about to get off, with none of her things ready, and she was *that* tired and sleepy she had not heard a word of the sermon. Grace really had undertaken too much. The house was in such a mess there was no sitting down quiet and respectable, and there was threepence in the till that would not be accounted for, and she was sure that the cheese was going too fast." She fretted all the way home, and Jessie could not comfort her, by promising to look over the accounts the first thing on Monday.

However, on coming home they found the whole house tidied, dinner laid, the pie made and just ready to come out of the Dutch oven, and the accounts balanced and written out fairly. Grace was just finishing the arraying herself in full Sunday trim outside, but how was it with the inner Sunday raiment of her heart?

She did nothing but talk about "seam and gusset and band," and how fast she was getting on, and how good the linen was, and what sort was the best, till Jessie thought she might almost as well have been sewing all day as with her thoughts running on nothing else.

When Jessie went to afternoon school, both Mrs. Hollis and Grace were so tired that the one went to sleep in her chair, and the other on her bed; and thus Jessie found them on her return.

Poor mother! how weary and worn her face looked after this week of worry. The sight of it settled Jessie's mind. She went up softly to take off her things, and as she was doing so, Grace awoke. Jessie went up to her and showed her Miss Needwood's cipher.

43

"Bless me! whose is that? It is real genteel," said Grace.

"It is Miss Needwood's at Chalk-pit Farm."

"What! that poor helpless thing that never can keep a situation! Did you get it for a pattern, Jessie?"

"Yes," said Jessie; "she lent it to me."

"It is beautiful," said Grace, examining it minutely. "You ought to work like that, Jessie."

"I would if I could," said Jessie, "and I mean to try; but, Grace, I shall only finish this first dozen. I shall send the other five dozen to Bessie Needwood. She is in great want of work, and will do them much better than I."

"Well I never!" cried Grace. "I never thought you'd turn lazy, and give up what you had undertaken—when I had asked for the handkerchiefs on purpose for you, because I thought a little pocket money would come in convenient!"

"So it would. It was very kind of you, Grace; but Miss Needwood will do them better than I."

"Not than you if you chose to take the pains and trouble."

"No," said Jessie, "if I don't hurry them too quick to try to do those finest stitches, I sha'n't have time to do them at all, in these after hours of mine."

"Well, that you should choose to confess yourself not able to do as well as a poor dozing thing like that! It's all laziness."

"No, that it is not," said Jessie, rather hotly. "I thought if those were off my hands I could help you, and then mother need not have any of this work to do, or be so driven and put about."

"You don't expect to be paid for any part of mother's work," said Grace, with some sharpness. "I've got my own use for that in the business."

"No, I don't!" and Jessie went suddenly off in a little bit of temper for which she was sorry afterwards, wishing she had said that her real reason— besides the helping Miss Needwood—was the hope to save her mother from being over driven, and not to have another Sunday so cumbered with worldly matters.

Grace came down to tea grumbling, and appealing to her mother about Jessie's laziness; and Mrs. Hollis, for whose sake the girl had resigned five-sixths of her hoped-for gain, was inclined to be vexed at any of the work going out of the family, or her Jessie allowing herself to be beaten.

It was very vexatious, and Jessie was glad when Uncle Andrew dropped in to tea, and to change the current of their thoughts.

She was to stay at home to guard the house while the others went to evensong, and this gave her the quiet opportunity of packing up five dozen handkerchiefs, and writing a note to send with them to Bessie Needwood the first thing in the morning, by any child who came early to the shop.

Then she felt much more at ease, and was able to have a comfortable study of her next Sunday's Gospel and its references, in case she should be too busy on the week days; and so she was peaceful and refreshed, and able to enjoy a quiet little wander in the twilight garden with her hymn-book. This lasted till the others came home, brim full of reports they had picked up about the splendour of the coming wedding. The gentleman, Mr. Holdaway, was staying at Newcorn Park, and, what was more, he had sent his horses and grooms down to the Manners Arms, because the stables at the Chequers were not well kept.

The head groom had actually been at Church, and looked quite the gentleman, though to be sure he did stare about wonderfully.

Mrs. Hollis shook her head, and said no good came of that sort of folk.

CHAPTER VII.

WANDERING EYES.

"I ASSURE you he said he had never seen a place with more pretty young ladies in it."

"Who?" said Jessie, coming suddenly into the light closet of the work-room, where Florence Cray was taking off her hat, and Amy Lee seemed to be helping her.

"Why, Mr. Wingfield, Mr. Holdaway's head groom, who has come over with another man and a boy, and three of the loveliest horses you ever did see."

"Oh, yes, I heard," said Jessie; "and how he stared about at Church! He ought to be ashamed of himself."

"Oh! that's what Grace says, of course," said Florence; "and she's a regular old maid. She needn't fear that he'll stare at her."

Wherewith both Florence and Amy giggled, and before Jessie's hot answer was out of her mouth, one of the aunts called out—

"Girls, girls, what are you doing? No gossiping there."

Florence came out looking cross, and observing in a marked manner that Miss Fuller, at Ellerby, always spoke of her young ladies.

"I like using right names," said Aunt Rose in her decided voice.

Florence was silenced for the time, but at the dinner hour she contrived to get Amy alone. Jessie was in haste to get home to see if there were an answer from Miss Needwood, and also to try to get enough sewing done to pacify Grace, and purchase a little leisure for her mother. And Florence, instead of going home, stood with Amy, who had sauntered into the garden to refresh herself and gather some parsley.

"I assure you, Amy, he was quite struck. He said yours was such a style that he would hardly believe me when I said you belonged to Mr. Lee, the baker. It was the refinement, he said."

"Nonsense, Florence; don't," said Amy, blushing as crimson as the rose she tried to gather.

"I'm not talking nonsense; I never did see a poor man so smitten."

"Now, Florence, you shouldn't say such things; father and aunts would not like it. I shall go in."

"Fathers and aunts are all alike; they never do like such things. But——"

However, Amy was safe indoors by this time, all in a glow, very much ashamed that such things should have been said to her, and yet not a little fluttered and pleased. She had been most carefully brought up and watched over, and she had come to the age of sixteen without hearing more about herself than that a young lady, who once came into the school with Miss Agnes Manners, said something that sounded like lovely, and was speedily hushed up and silenced.

All the other girls thought the young lady meant Henrietta Coles, who was tall, with bright dark eyes, red cheeks, and black hair, under a round comb; but Amy had always been sure that the speaker's eyes were upon her, though she had been ashamed of the belief, and indeed had nearly forgotten all about it, till it was stirred up by Florence's talk.

She went up to her room to smooth her hair before dinner. Yes, it was very nice light-brown hair, with a golden shine; and her eyes were very clear and blue, and her skin very white, with a rosy flush; and her nose was straight, and the shape was a pretty delicate one. Amy really did think Mr. Wingfield was right, and had better taste than the people who thought her a poor washy, peaky thing, as she had more than once heard herself called.

She put her head on one side, smirked a little, half shut her eyes, and studied herself in different positions, till she heard one of her aunts on the stairs; and then, in a desperate fright lest she should be caught, she darted out so fast as to run against Aunt Charlotte coming up stairs with a basket of clean linen from the wash. There were three pairs of stockings rolled up on the top, and these tumbled out, and one pair went hop, hop, from step to step all the way down stairs, just as Father was coming in, and he caught it up and threw it like a ball straight up at his sister.

The confusion drove the nonsense out of Amy's head for the present. She ate her dinner, and then went off as usual for her visit to little Edwin Smithers, carrying him only a few strawberries, as she knew he always had soup from the Hall on a Monday.

For Edwin had not died. He had rather grown better than worse, and if the truth must be told, Amy had begun to get a little tired of him. He was not a quick child, and in this hot weather he often failed to do the sums or learn the verses that Amy set him.

To-day he was nursing a great piece of stick-liquorice with which he had painted a dirty spot on the central face in the picture of the number of the *Chatterbox* which she had lent him. She scolded him for it, and he turned sulky, and would not try to repeat his hymn, nor answer any questions, and looked at his book as if he had never seen one before.

Amy grew angry, told him he was a naughty boy, and she should not stay with him nor give him any strawberries; and off she went, carrying away the injured *Chatterbox*, and never bethinking herself that the hot day and the weariness of the dull untidy room might not be the cause of the naughty fit, and whether it would not have been kinder and better to try to soothe him out of it.

But instead of this she paused to hear Mrs. Rowe declare he was a bad 'un, with a nasty sulky temper that no one could do nothing with, and just then she saw Florence Cray crossing the village green.

"I've just been to get a little red pepper at Hollis's," she said, as she put her arm fondly into Amy's. "Mr. Wingfield do like something tasty for his breakfast, and ma is going to do him some devilled kidneys to-morrow morning. He is quite the gentleman in all his tastes, you see! I wanted Jessie to walk back with me, but they are all so terrible busy over that there wedding order, that she could not come till the last minute."

"Working all through the dinner hour!" said Amy. "What a shame!"

"So I say. But that Grace Hollis is a one! I wouldn't have her for my sister. Here, come in, Amy, I must just give mother the pepper."

"No, I can't do that," said Amy, uneasily, for she knew her father would be displeased if she went into a public-house; though as Florence said, "Gracious! You needn't go near the bar. It's only the back door! As if I would ask you to do anything you ought not! But I suppose our house ain't good enough for you."

"Oh! don't be angry, Florence dear, I'll come some day when I've got leave."

"Leave indeed, at your age; but you're a poor-spirited thing, Amy, to be so kept down by a couple of old aunts."

Amy was flurried at the displeasure, and wanted to make it up. "Oh! don't be offended, Florence. Look here."

"Strawberries! oh my! already! Thank you," and Florence had soon swallowed up poor little Edwin's strawberries.

"Wait here one moment then," she said, "and I'll be back with you in an instant."

49

Amy stood under her parasol, trying to make the most of the small shelter afforded by Mr. Cray's garden hedge, and recollecting rather uncomfortably something she had once been told about the loitering of the disobedient Prophet being what brought him into temptation. But, having promised to wait, she could not move away, though she had to stay longer than she liked, especially as the children were going by to afternoon school, and some of her own class began to stare at her.

However, at last Florence came out, quite excited. "Oh, Amy, if you'll only wait a minute, you'll see him come out."

"I can't! I can't! Let us go," cried Amy, quite shocked and shy.

"Nonsense! Poor man, he need never see you. He is just going to take the horses up for his master to ride out with Miss Robson. Such sweet horses! Mr. Holdaway gave 120 guineas for his. Think of that, Amy! Here now, come round the corner of the hedge, and he'll never see you."

So Amy followed and peeped, very shy and frightened, like a guilty thing, and she did see two horses, much more beautiful than she knew, one ridden by a common-looking groom, the other by a very smart, well set-up person, with a belt round his waist. That was all she saw, for they were gone in a flash, and she was too uncomfortable to see much, or to do more than hurriedly answer Florence's exclamation—

"Ain't he quite the gentleman? Bain't his horses real darlings?" before Jessie's voice was heard—

"Why, whatever are you two doing here?"

The two girls both giggled, and each pushed the other to make her tell, and Florence laughed out—

"Oh, 'twas Amy wanted to see Mr. Wingfield pass by."

"No, 'twasn't. 'Twas you," said Amy.

"I don't see why you should get into a corner about it," said Jessie, rather gravely. "I've just met him straight upon the road, horses and all."

"O yes, *you*!" said Florence.

"Well, why not me?"

"O, you know, you'll soon be an old maid like your sister."

Jessie had not grown so wise as not to be nettled at this silly impertinent speech, but she was much more vexed to see that Florence was teaching Amy her own follies—Amy, who had always seemed like a pure little innocent wild rose-bud in its modest green leaves. So she answered, rather shortly—

"If you mean that I don't want to be right down ridiculous, I hope I am an old maid."

This seemed to be very funny, for Florence went off in fits of laughing, and kept shouldering Amy to make her see the joke, but Amy had by this time grown ashamed and frightened and only answered, "Don't."

So the three girls went in together, and no one took any special notice of Amy's hot face and uncomfortable gestures. It was the first time since she had been a very little child that she had shrunk from her aunts' eyes, or feared that they should ask her questions; and the sense that she had been undeserving of the trust they placed in her made her very ill at ease, though the silly girl did not do the only thing that would have set her right again, and made her safer for the future.

Jessie meanwhile had forgotten the little vexation. She had something to brighten her up in Miss Needwood's little note.

It was written on pink paper, edged with blue, as if nothing could be too good for Jessie; and it said no words could tell how glad she was, and what a comfort it was to have this real work to do. "It is really like a ray of hope in the darkness," said poor Bessie, in her little thin weak writing, with a very hard steel pen.

But that note warmed up Jessie's heart, although her finger was getting severely ploughed up with the stitching she had been doing to save her mother's eyes.

"There was not to be an inch of machine work," Mrs. Robson had said, and the Hollises were people who fulfilled all they undertook.

But Jessie's hour at home had helped and freshened her mother, who looked much less worn and worried than she had done the day before. Jessie felt she had done well to send away the handkerchiefs, and lessen the burthen Grace had taken upon the family.

CHAPTER VIII.

AMY'S VISITS.

NOBODY could say any great harm of Florence Cray, or she would not have been bound to Miss Lee.

But she was one of those silly, vulgar-minded girls who think life is nothing without continually chattering either to young men or about them. She was in no hurry to be married, for then she knew she must give up all her lively pastime with the lads around her. Not that she frequented the bar, or had anything to do with the customers—her mother kept her carefully from that; but she had plenty of acquaintance, and to her mind nothing else was so amusing. She was not pretty, and knew it well enough, but she was very good-natured, and free from jealousy, and next to diverting herself with some youth, she liked nothing so well as teasing other girls about them.

She considered Amy Lee quite old enough and pretty enough to have a young man, and to begin to have some fun, and she thought all the care taken of the girl by her father and aunts only so much stupid old fidget and jealousy, which it was fun to baffle and elude. Thus she was a very dangerous companion for Amy, perhaps more so than a really worse person, who would have been more shocking and startling to Amy's sense of modesty and propriety. It was such a new sensation altogether to be always popping about and peeping to admire the handsome stranger and his fine horses, and then to whisk giggling out of the way, in terror lest they had been seen.

It was more amusing than sitting by a fretful boy, trying to make him read and say hymns, and though conscience was half awake, it was easily satisfied. And then there was the pleasure of being told that she was admired—though Amy would not have liked it as well if she had guessed that Florence used to amuse herself on the other hand by telling Mr. Wingfield how a certain young lady admired him, and teasing him by declaring that, "Oh no! she could not tell him who, she should be nameless. Did he like best fair or dark?"

So time went on, and the needlework with it. Grace Hollis's whole brain seemed to be turning into thread and cotton, for she was able to think of nothing else except what she should do with the money, when she got it; but she did not scold Jessie, as she had been inclined to do at first, for giving up the handkerchiefs, for she had begun to find that without her sister's help there would have been no chance of finishing, without overworking her mother, and neglecting the business of the shop.

Indeed, as it was, when the last week came there was so much still to be done that she was obliged to ask Miss Needwood to come and help, which she was very glad to do, when she had finished the handkerchiefs most delicately and beautifully.

Jessie gave all the time she could. She was glad to have something to think about, for Miss Manners was from home, so there were no readings before the Sundays; and her sharp eyes could not help seeing that there was something underhand going on between Amy and Florence—where she did not know whether to interfere or not.

She had seen Amy and Florence come hastily round the corner of the lane, which had a stile into a large shady path field at the back of Mrs. Smithers's cottage, and Mr. Wingfield hovering about. It did not look well—and indeed what she would have thought nothing of in such a girl as Florence was a very different thing in Amy. Then stories that she disliked were afloat about the man. He was said to be teaching the young men at the Manners Arms new gambling games, and to be putting them up to bet on race-horses; and once she heard a very unpleasant laugh about very good, closely-kept girls being as ready to carry on as other folk.

Once when she asked Amy after little Edwin Smithers, the answer was rather cross. "Oh! just as usual. He is the most tiresome fractious child I ever saw!"

"Children are often like that when they are going to be worse," said Jessie.

"Well," returned Amy, "I've always heard that children are most fretty and fussy when they are getting better."

"Then I hope he is better."

"O dear yes, of course he is, or he would not be here now," said Amy, impatiently, and getting very red.

"How does he get on with his reading?"

"There never was such a one for questions as you, Jessie!" cried Amy, getting quite cross.

And as Jessie knew curiosity to be her failing, and was really trying to break herself of it, she was silenced.

No doubt Amy was angered because her conscience was very far from being easy, though she never failed to pop into the Smithers's cottage every day, sometimes to bring the little dainties her aunts provided, sometimes to say a few words and begin a lesson with Edwin; but her heart was not in it, the boy would seldom attend, and often turned away his face and said "No," or began to cry; whereupon Amy told him he was very naughty, and marched off, excusing herself by the fact that the girl Polly was generally in the house, and seemed to be attending to him much better than she used to do.

No wonder Amy was in a hurry, for Florence was waiting for her outside; and by and by not only Florence.

It began one windy day when Amy's sunshade flew out of her hand. She ran after it, as it went dancing along on its spokes over the village green, jumping up just as she neared it, and whisking off just as if it had been alive, or like one of those gay butterflies and birds in allegories that lure the little pilgrims out of the narrow path. Alas! it was only too much like such a deluder.

For some one came round the corner, caught the wild sunshade, and restored it to the owner. She was tittering and breathless, she blushed all over, and never raised her eyes while Mr. Wingfield hoped, in elegant language, that she had not fatigued herself, and paid a flattering compliment to the lovely colour with which exercise had suffused her complexion. This made her giggle and blush all the more. She did not know whether she liked it or not, poor silly child!

She often "wished he would not;" she was in a dreadful fright whenever it happened, and yet the day seemed flat and tiresome and not worth having when he had not joined her and Florence, and walked down the path below Hornbeam Wood, behind Mrs. Smithers's cottage, with them.

He never said or did anything to startle her. He saw she was a modest, well-behaved girl, and he knew how to treat such a one. He talked chiefly about the preparations for the wedding, or made the two simple country girls stare by wonderful stories of the horses he had ridden and driven, or by descriptions of the parks and the theatre. Now and then he was complimentary, but Florence told Amy much more of his admiration than she ever heard herself. As to letting her father or aunts know of the acquaintance, Amy was half afraid, half ashamed. One day she heard a talk between her father and Mr. Nowell, the gardener at the Hall, who was vexed about an under gardener.

"I shall have to speak to the Squire about him, I am afraid," said Mr. Nowell; "he don't do his work with half a heart, and instead of spending his evenings at the club, or at cricket—wholesome and hearty like—he is always down at Cray's."

"I hear," said Mr. Lee, "the club was never so badly attended."

"They say it is all along of that there smart groom, Wingfield, as they call him, who is all for gambling games, and putting up our young lads to betting tricks and the like."

"Ay, ay," said Mr. Lee, "one of them idle, good-for-nothing servants loafing about at a public will do more harm in a place than you can undo in a day."

"That's true," added Aunt Rose; "I can't bear the sight of the fellow lounging about with his little stick, as if he was saying to all the place, 'Here I am; it's just improvement to you all to see how I switch my legs.'"

"And he stares so!" added Aunt Charlotte. "Last time Amy and I met him on the road, I really thought he would have stared the poor child out of countenance. I had a great mind to have spoken to him, and told him to mind his manners."

"You are too young and too good-looking to do that sort of thing, Charlotte," said her brother, laughing. "May be 'twas your aunt he looked at, so you needn't go as red as a turkey-cock, Amy girl."

"Me, indeed!" said Charlotte, in hot indignation. "I should hope I was *past* being stared at by a whipper-snapper monkey like that."

The elders all laughed heartily, and Mr. Nowell said something about Miss Charlotte being a fine woman of her time of life, which made her still more angry, and set her brother and sister laughing the more.

Amy squeezed out a weak little giggle, but she was both angered and frightened. She could never tell her aunts now. What would they say? The time of the wedding was drawing on; Mr. Wingfield would be going. Little flutters moved her breast. Would he say any more before he went, or did she wish it? Florence said he was dying for her. Florence thought he was a gentleman in disguise, like one she had read about in a novel; but Amy, though she liked to dream of something sweet and grand years hence, did not want to be startled by love-making now, or to have the dreadful disturbance at home there would be if this were more than a summer acquaintance. How would the aunts look, when they found she had concealed all this—she who had never hidden anything from them before?

And yet she took the stolen pleasure in trembling every day, and tried to believe Florence when she said there was no harm in it, that every one did so, and that young people must be young!

CHAPTER IX.

AWKWARD MEETINGS.

"WELL, to be sure, who would have thought of such a treat! This is a pleasure indeed! Rose, Rose, whom do you think we have here?"

"How natural it all do look to be sure. There, Ambrose, there's the very rose tree I have so often told you of."

"Why, mother has described it all so well, I could have found my way blindfold."

The speaker was a tall, fair-faced young man, looking, in Charlotte Lee's eyes, like one of the young gentlemen from the university, but with something grave and deep about his face, and by him stood his little mother in the neatest of black silk dresses, with something sweet and childlike about her face still, though there were some middle-aged lines in it. She had once been the Amy Lee of Langley. She had married a schoolmaster, Mr. Cuthbert, and this was their only son. He had distinguished himself in all his examinations, and at the same time had shown so deep an interest in missions to the heathen, and had done so much to make the boys of the school care for them, that when there was a question of choosing a lad as a missionary student, whose expenses would be paid by subscriptions of the clergy in the diocese, at the great college of St. Augustine's at Canterbury, the vicar of his parish had three years ago proposed Ambrose Cuthbert as the fittest youth he knew. He had just finished his terms at the college, and was on his way home before going out to Rupertsland, having met his mother at the house of his father's brother in London. They had found out that an excursion train would enable them to run down to Langley and spend a few hours there; and Mrs. Cuthbert, who had always said her son must not leave England without having seen her old home, her brother and sisters, was delighted with the opportunity, and here they were, the brother and the three sisters all together, hardly knowing what they said in their eager joy.

"And my little Amy, where is she? You have not seen your namesake, Amy," said the father, who had come in bare armed and floury.

"She is not come back yet from poor little Teddy's," said Aunt Rose. "The child goes to teach, and see to, a poor little sick lad in a cottage every day, Amy. We like her to do such things," she added, pleased that her sister should see that their child was likewise something superior in goodness. "Ah! is it you, Jessie? This is Clemmy Fielding's daughter, Amy. Did you see our Amy as you came along, Jessie?"

"I will run back and call her," said Jessie, who had seen the top of Amy's sunshade over the hedge, and in good-natured sympathy wanted to spare all the shock of discovery.

"No, no," said Miss Rose, "thank you all the same, Jessie, but if you would not mind sitting down to the machine, I would walk out that way with my sister, just while my brother is finishing his batch of bread, and you are getting ready a bit of something to eat, Charlotte. I know, Amy, you would like just to look round the hill, and see where the squire's new cottages lie. Wouldn't you?"

Jessie saw there was no help for it. Mrs. Cuthbert was delighted to go and to show her son her old haunts; but first she spoke very kindly to Jessie, and inquired for her mother, saying she remembered her well; and on her side Jessie recollected that her mother always said she owed more to Mrs. Cuthbert's kindness when she was a little girl than to any one else.

So off set the two elder sisters and the pleasant looking young man together. Amy always was late, and Jessie felt one hope, that they might meet the two girls coming in together. Yet, as she whirred her machine, she reflected that after all it might be best for Amy in the end that all this folly and concealment should be put a stop to.

Out they went, talking; Mrs. Cuthbert asking questions, and pointing everything out to her son, and Aunt Rose delighted to answer.

"We do not hurry the maid," said Aunt Rose, as they drew near. "You see it is such a blessing to that poor little afflicted child to have her with him."

Perhaps Rose Lee, who had had her dreams and fancies like other people, was thinking of the tales where some one looks in at the window and sees the good young person bending over the sufferer's couch, and reading good books to him; but it was certainly not Amy whom she saw as the door stood open. There was the little boy on the old couch under the window, moaning a little, but it was his sister who was standing by him with a cup of something, coaxing him with "Now Teddy, do be a good boy, and drink it, do'ee now."

"Why, Polly," said Aunt Rose, "are you here?"

"Please, Miss Lee," said Polly, in a high squeaky voice of self-defence, "Our Ted is so bad, I couldn't go to school, not this afternoon."

"And where's Miss Amy? Not gone for the doctor?" asked Rose, seeing indeed that the poor child looked very ill.

"No, miss," said Polly. "Teacher Amy don't come now for more than a minute."

"Where is she then?" asked Rose, to whom the world seemed whirling round; while Ambrose Cuthbert stood at the door, and his mother was feeling the poor child's hands, and looking with dismay at the grease gathering on the half cold broth with which his sister had been trying to feed him.

But Polly's answer was quite ready—"Down the mead along with that there Wingfield and Cray's gal."

"Who?" asked Rose, severely, for the girl's tone had that sort of pert simplicity, or simple pertness, that children can put on when they know they are giving unpleasant information, but will not seem to understand it.

"With Mr. Wingfield, the gentleman's groom up at the Arms," said she. "He be her young man."

Ambrose Cuthbert turned his head outwards to hide a smile. Rose said hotly, "Hold your tongue, child! don't be saucy! Come, Amy, here is some mistake."

"Stay, Rose," said Mrs. Cuthbert, "the child is really very ill. Has he a mother? Something ought to be done."

Rose did not feel as if she could care for the boy at such a moment, and just then old Mrs. Rowe, brought by the sound of voices, came in by the back door.

"Ay! Rose Lee," she said. "If you wants to know where your fine niece is, just look here. I never knew no good come of bringing up young folks to be better than their neighbours, going about a visiting as if they was ladies."

Rose had reached the back garden, and over the broken-down little gate she saw—in the path shaded by the coppice—three figures whom she knew only too well, sauntering towards the stile leading into the lane.

She felt quite giddy, as she called out sharply, "Amy Lee!"

There was a great start. The three stood still, and looked about as if to see where the voice came from. Rose, recollecting the old woman's malicious eyes, got over the stile and came towards them. They had seen her by this time; she perceived that they were whispering; then the man retreated, and Florence and Amy came towards her, Florence holding Amy's hand, and pushing to the front.

"Miss Lee," she said, "we weren't doing no harm. Only taking a walk before coming in."

"Florence Cray," returned Miss Lee, "I don't want to have anything to say

60

to you. If you have been teaching Amy to deceive her father and me, so much the worse. You need not come to work this afternoon. My sister, Mrs. Cuthbert, is come to see us, so I shall not require you. Come here, Amy."

"You'll not be hard on her, Miss Lee," entreated good-natured Florence, feeling Amy's fingers cling to her. "I do assure you there's been nothing no one could except against. It's been all most prudent and proper all along."

"I said I don't wish to hear nothing from you," said Rose. "If you call it prudent and proper to be walking with young men, when she is trusted to read to a sick child, I don't know what I shall hear next. Come here, Amy; come home with me."

"Indeed, aunt," sobbed Amy, "I've been in every day to see him."

"Come home now, Amy," said her aunt; "I can't talk to you now! No, don't cry—don't speak! I won't have you making yourself a show to the whole place any more than you have done already. That you should have deceived us so!" she sighed to herself. She was taking Amy in, not by the garden, but round the corner of the lane, to give a little more time for her to recover herself, and also to avoid facing Mrs. Rowe's eager eyes.

"Please don't tell father," once sighed Amy.

"Do you think I am going to be as deceitful as yourself?" was all the answer she got.

Amy's was a meek nature, and she knew she had been doing very wrong, so she uttered no more entreaties; indeed, she was in such a trembling, choking state, that her aunt had to wait, and walk slowly, while the girl tried to control herself enough to appear respectably—in a little lurking hope that perhaps Aunt Rose would be better than her word, and at least not tell Aunt Amy, her godmother, or Cousin Ambrose. She, who had been always reckoned so good a girl, and had never been in disgrace before! That it should have happened at such a time!

And when the garden gate was opened, there was a further shock. More people were in the house! Miss Manners, who had come home the night before, had come to inquire for little Edwin, and there was a buzz of voices, as she and Mrs. Cuthbert had most joyfully greeted one another.

Miss Manners was delighted to see the young missionary, and the only drawback was that poor little Edwin was evidently so much worse. He had been gradually growing worse and weaker for the last ten days or a fortnight, Polly and Mrs. Rowe said, and his mother had sad nights with him; but the parish doctor had said it was only feverishness caused by the heat, when he saw the boy last week, and did not seem to think it of consequence. The family depended on the mother's work, and in hay-making time she could not stay at home. Mr. Somers was gone from home, so was Miss Manners, and no one had thought much about the poor child; but he had become so much worse in the course of the morning, that it was plain that his mother and the doctor must both be sent for without loss of time.

Miss Manners came out into the garden with Mrs. Cuthbert, and as the aunt and niece came up, said she would find the messenger.

"Had not you thought him so well, Amy?" she asked.

"Oh, ma'am!" exclaimed Aunt Rose, always an outspoken person, "that's the worst trouble of all! Who would have thought this sly deceitful child could have made as if she was sitting all the time with that poor boy, while she was just walking all the time with that good-for-nothing groom up at the Arms. How I shall tell her poor father, I don't know. It will be enough to break his heart!"

"It was all Florence Cray!" sobbed Amy.

"Well," said Miss Manners, "of course her father must know about it; but since Amy the elder is only to be here three or four hours, don't you think it would be better not to spoil her visit for him? You can have it out in the evening, you know; but it would be a great pity to give him such a shock at once. Don't you think so, Amy?"

"Indeed I do, ma'am," said Mrs. Cuthbert; "I am afraid the poor girl may have been to blame, but it will not be the worse for her to wait a little while, and my brother would be so much taken up with the matter, that I am afraid my Ambrose would never know his uncle as I should like."

"I'm sure it will all be spoilt to me, any way," said poor Aunt Rose, half choked.

"But you will bear the burthen alone, for your brother's sake and Charlotte's," said Miss Manners, cheerfully; "besides, you have your own dear old Amy to help you to bear it, and that is like old times."

This comforted Rose a good deal. Miss Dora—as she and her sister Amy still called her—said she would not say good-bye, she would look in before the Cuthberts went, and say how the child was.

The younger Amy was glad at first of the respite, but altogether it was the most dreadful day she ever spent. There was her father in his Sunday best coming out to meet them, wondering what had made them stay so long. Mrs. Cuthbert answered, to save Aunt Rose, that they had found the child much worse, and that Miss Manners had come in. This satisfied him, and they went in to the meal Aunt Charlotte had prepared—a very late luncheon, or early and solid tea, whichever it might be called—in the parlour, with the best china, and everything as nice as possible.

Really Amy felt as if it would have been less dreadful to have been locked up in her room, or sitting sewing with Jessie in the workroom, than sitting up in the parlour with the rest, and hearing her father show his pride in her, making her fetch her prize for the religious examination, and talking of her almost as if he wanted to compare her with Aunt Amy's missionary son.

And then when Ambrose Cuthbert was questioned about his plans, and told in a very modest quiet way where he was to go, and the work he was to do under a missionary to the Red Indians, Amy saw more and more how foolish she had been. What was that conceited groom whose boast was of the horses he had ridden, and the bets laid on them, compared with this young man? Which was the gentleman of the two? And this was her own first cousin, and she had forfeited the respect and esteem which he might have carried out with him! He would only—in those far countries—think of his cousin, Amy Lee, as a giddy, deceitful, hypocritical girl, who had carried on a flirtation under cover of a good work.

Amy burnt to tell all the excuses she thought she had, and how she had been led on, and that it was not so bad as no doubt Aunt Rose thought; but she must keep all back. Only at last her father remarked that his darling was very silent—shy, he thought, with her grand scholarly cousin. He said he should like them to hear what a pretty voice she had, and told her to sing one of her hymns, such as "Abide with us;" but Amy could not do that. She put her face in her hands, choked, and began to cry.

"Ah!" said Aunt Charlotte; "poor dear, it has been a great shock to her, the poor little boy being taken so much worse."

It was a comfort to every one that at that moment Miss Manners came in through the shop, asking for Jessie Hollis.

"The poor little boy is very ill," she said. "The only thing that seems to soothe him is a bit of a verse that his sister Mary says her teacher taught her. That was you—is it not, Jessie? Mary can only say half, and we can't make it out; but she says, 'If teacher was but here.'"

Of course Miss Lee was ready to spare Jessie for such a reason, and she folded up her work while Miss Manners had a little talk with Mrs. Cuthbert, on the mingled pain and sweetness of the giving up her only son to be one of those sent forth "to sow beside all waters."

"I am so glad he should have seen you, ma'am, before he leaves us," said his mother, the tears rising in her quiet eyes. "I only wish he could have seen Miss Edith—Mrs. Howard; for indeed, ma'am, I always feel that whatever good my children have learnt at home, was owing to the way I was brought up and the way Miss Edith used to talk to us."

"Nothing will make my sister so happy as to hear it, Amy," said Miss Manners. "Somehow it seems to chime in with what I had ventured to bring as a little remembrance of your old home for your son. I had prepared it to send the St. Augustine's scholar, before I knew I should see him."

She gave him a beautiful little *Christian Year* and *Lyra Innocentium* in a case together, and as the book-marker was the illuminated text—

> "In the morning sow thy seed,
> And in the evening withhold not thine hand,
> For thou knowest not which shall prosper."

Ambrose Cuthbert thanked the lady in a very nice way, telling her that he should value her gift much, and that he hoped to make the poems his companions and often his guides in his work.

So with a warm pressure of the hands of both mother and son, Miss

Manners walked away with Jessie.

"I think," she presently said, "some of your bread on the waters is coming back to you, Jessie. They say that little Mary Smithers has been such a comfort to her little brother, by repeating to him what she learns on Sundays, and that she has been so much more good and attentive to him of late."

"I am sure, ma'am," said Jessie, "I never thought Mary Smithers seemed to understand anything."

"We can never judge where the seed we sow will prosper," said Miss Dora, thinking within herself of the different results with Amy and Jessie.

The little boy had been carried up to the bedroom. Old Mrs. Rowe was there, and his mother, who was trying to help him to lie more easily, while he moved feebly, but restlessly, and still looked at little Polly, who was repeating over and over some verse in which "Shepherd" was the only word that Miss Manners, well as she knew the children's tones, could make out. Jessie, however, knew it directly, and repeated—

> "Gracious Saviour, gentle Shepherd,
>   Little ones are dear to Thee,
> Gathered in Thine Arms and carried,
>   In Thy Bosom may we be
> Sweetly, fondly, gently tended,
>   From all want and danger free."

She could say the whole hymn, but the child grew restless as soon as she had passed beyond the first verse. She returned to it, once, twice, and then Polly got back what she had partly forgotten and went on with it, which was evidently what quieted the boy best. He seemed too far gone to attend to anything else; the sense of other words did not reach his ears, but these evidently gave him pleasure. The doctor had said he was dying, and the women thought he would sleep himself away. There seemed no more to be done. Polly had her verse to say to him, and no help seemed needed; so Miss Manners and Jessie went down the stairs again, and out into the garden, Jessie shedding many tears, but very far from sad ones. When she could speak, she said that the young woman in the hospital to whom she owed so much knew the hymn, and had so often repeated it, that Jessie had learnt it. She had used the first verse one Sunday when teaching the children about the Good Shepherd, and, having a little more time than usual, had tried to teach it to them—little thinking how she should thus meet it—but using it because she had grown fond of it for the sake of her friend, and of the new and higher feelings that were linked with the first learning of it.

There was a great peace and thankfulness in her heart at having thus tasted a sort of first-fruits of her little attempt at sowing. It was soothing a death- bed! Might not she well rejoice that she had persevered, in spite of the temptation of gain, in not letting her head and heart be carried away with the fever of work, but giving the best part of herself to the task she had undertaken?

Not that Jessie saw or thought that this had been the case. Yet if she had let herself be swept away with Grace's vehement desire to engross all the needlework, she must have given up her preparation; she would have been wearied, hurried, and very likely fretful and impatient. At any rate, there would not have been that kindness and earnestness which leads others to be good far more than the actual words of teaching.

CHAPTER X.

THE RECKONING.

"I<small>T</small> is a right punishment for our sinful pride in her," said Aunt Rose, as she had a few last words alone with her elder sister.

"Well, Rose," said Mrs. Cuthbert, "I would not be so very hard on the poor child. I've been watching her, and I think, though no doubt she has done very wrong, it was in a childish sort of way, and that you won't find there's been any real love-making or nonsense of that sort."

"I'm sure, now I find the child could deceive us so, and act such a part, there's nothing I could not believe," said poor Aunt Rose.

"That is sad enough, but I think you'll find it the worst, and that she was led into it by others."

"That Florence Cray!" exclaimed Rose; "and what to do about her? How hinder her from spoiling our child, when she's bound apprentice to me? I wish I'd never listened to her father!"

Here came Amy herself, sent up to say that the trap was ready, and her aunt must not be late for the train. She felt as if the last protection was gone when she saw her aunt and cousin driven away in the conveyance they had hired at Ellerby.

Girls bred up like Florence Cray would have thought it all a great fuss about nothing. First and last Florence had seen nothing but fun in Amy's cheating her strait-laced aunts and getting a little diversion, while they wanted to shut her up with a cross child; but Amy had been bred up to a very different way of looking at things, and the whole afternoon had only been setting more fully before her how she had fallen from what she had imagined of herself last Lent!

After all, the delay had made it better for her. Aunt Rose did not tell the story quite so hotly and violently as it would have come out in the first shock of wrath, but it was dreadful enough to hear her father say—

"Amy, child, what is this? I never thought you would go for to do such a thing."

"You that we had trusted from a baby," added Aunt Rose.

Aunt Charlotte said nothing, but her looks were the worst of all to bear, they were so gentle and so sorrowful. And when Amy had sobbed out her story they told her that she had been so sly that they did not know how to believe her word.

"Oh, father! you may believe me. I never told a story—no, I never did!"

"And yet you could make as if you were going day by day to sit with that poor little chap, only that you might be tramping about the lanes with that there scamp!"

It was what he took as the hypocrisy of the thing that chiefly wounded Mr. Lee, and when Amy declared she had always gone into the cottage and spoken to the boy, she was told, "Much she could have attended to him, since she had never seen that the poor child was dying."

The fact was that Florence had hurried her a good deal, because Mr. Wingfield was to show them the rosettes the horses were to wear on the wedding-day.

After all, Amy had to go up to her room only half believed and unforgiven. Her father had a great mind to have gone to have had it out with Florence Cray that night, but as some holiday people were there, he doubted whether he could see her alone, and waited till the morning. Then he called her into the parlour and said:

"Florence Cray, what have you been doing with my girl?"

"No harm, Mr. Lee," said Florence, frightened, but therefore pert, and resolved to stand up for her friend. "You may trust me for that! I know what is proper."

Mr. Lee made an odd sort of noise, and said: "You do, eh! Proper to deceive her friends—"

"Oh! now, Mr. Lee," said Florence, looking up in the droll, saucy way that served her instead of beauty, "it was only two old aunts. One always reckons it fair play by an old aunt."

"Have done with nonsense like that," said Mr. Lee. "Now, Florence Cray, mine is a girl with no mother. My sisters, and I have done our best to keep her a good, innocent girl, and we can't but feel it a hard thing that you should come leading her to keep company, without our knowledge, with a fellow that you must know is not such as we would approve."

"I'm sure I meant no harm," said Florence, beginning to cry; "I only thought it was dull for her, and took her for a walk. And you needn't be afraid, Mr. Lee, I never left them alone not one minute, nor he never said one word; nor did more than just shake hands. You may trust me, Mr. Lee."

On the whole the Lees were satisfied that the mischief had not gone as far as such imprudence might have led. Mr. Wingfield would be gone in a few days, for the wedding was coming on, and Amy was certainly not in love with him. When she compared him with Ambrose Cuthbert, she felt sick of having been flattered for a moment by his attentions, and looked on the whole with the bitterest shame, as having led her away from all her good resolutions, and made her thus deceive and disobey her father and aunts. And when the knell rang for poor little Edwin Smithers she cried more than ever, feeling almost guilty of his death.

She never wished for a moment to accept the invitation for which she had once been so eager, to see Miss Robson's wedding clothes and wedding presents. Grace Hollis went and took Jessie, and Florence Cray went too.

These were a sight! Such gilt clocks! Such extraordinary contrivances for ink-stands, toilette apparatus, dinner services, and every service that could be thought of! Such girdles, chatelaines, rings and bracelets! Such silks and satins! such garments for morning, noon, and night, and even afternoon tea! And oh! such dressing-gowns!

They sent Florence Cray home thinking over all the novels she had ever seen, where a girl at an inn married a rich man, and also thinking how to alter her best hat.

They sent Grace Hollis home deep in plans how to get another order for plain work.

And they sent home, Jessie very happy indeed, for a lady's-maid had asked whether a dozen more handkerchiefs could be marked with "Maude" in the same style as the Nina.

Miss Needwood was really getting quite prosperous.

The next day, almost every one, who could, went to see as much as possible of the wedding; so Aunt Rose had not yet to endure the presence of Florence, and to keep watch that she did not chatter to Amy, who was drooping and shame-stricken enough.

That morning came a letter from Mrs. Cuthbert. She said she should be lonesome without Ambrose; and would her brother lend her his Amy for a few weeks, when she would do her best for the child, and not let her forget her needlework? This made things much easier to all; but Amy knew it was a very different going from home from what it might have been.

Before she came back, Florence Cray had found what she called "working at Old Lee's" so dull, that she had teased her parents into requesting the return of part of her premium, and binding her to the chief milliner in Ellerby.

CHAPTER XI.

WHICH SHALL PROSPER?

Mr. Somers had come home from his six weeks' holiday, and was talking over the village news with Miss Manners.

She told him of little Edwin Smithers's death, of the summons to Jessie Hollis, and of the visit of Mrs. Cuthbert.

"Of course it is wrong to judge," she said, "but do you remember that Lenten sermon, and the impression I told you it made?"

"I remember well. It was on the seed, and on bringing forth fruit."

"Well, when we had the Parable of the Sower the other day, I could not help thinking how it had worked out. There were some, like that Cray girl, who never seemed to take it in at all, but left it as something outside of them. Then three distinctly were moved to undertake something, the two Hollises and Amy Lee. Well, Grace dropped her missionary needlework as soon as that wedding order come in her way——"

"Don't be hard on her, Dora."

"No; but I'm afraid I can't help seeing that she does not seem to keep up her Sunday ways as she used. Then there's a sharp, worn, fretted way. I am very much afraid she is getting choked with the thorns."

"I don't know Miss Hollis well," he said, thoughtfully, "but I am afraid she does not look much beyond her shop."

"And my poor little Amy Lee responding so readily—seeming all that could be wished, and then showing herself so little able to stand temptation from that silly girl."

"I hope there was no more than silliness."

"I don't think there was; but still, after all the care Rose and Charlotte have taken to bring up that girl really refined, it was very disappointing to find her ready to be led away in an instant by foolish, vulgar admiration; above all, when it led her to neglect the good work she was supposed to be doing, it showed such shallowness."

"It is a comfort that often trials, and even falls, do deepen the soil, so that the roots may have a better hold another time," said Mr. Somers. "I think there is good hope that so it will be with poor little Amy. And I think you have some good soil to tell me of."

"Indeed I have. I am sure Jessie Hollis has shown herself good soil, and her work upon that very unpromising Mary Smithers showed itself remarkably. But that was not all I was thinking of. It seems to me that we have had a glimpse of what the hundredfold produce may be. Think of my dear sister Edith, working away at her class when there was much less help than now, and see what some of them have grown up, especially Amy Cuthbert. I know she had a good home, and other helps; but still I heard what she said of Edith's teaching and training. It has helped her to make that young Ambrose Cuthbert what he is,—and what may not be his harvest!"

"As though a man should cast seed into the field," said Mr. Somers, thoughtfully. "First the blade, then the ear, after that the full corn in the ear."

"Ah! I am leaping on too fast. We only see a little of the first-fruits," said Miss Manners, "and take it for an earnest of the rest." And then she repeated Bishop Heber's hymn, which she had often taught the children:—

"O God, by Whom the seed is given,
    By Whom the harvest blest,
  Whose Word, like manna showers from heaven,
    Is planted in our breast.

"Preserve it from the passing feet,
    From plunderers of the air,
  The sultry sun's intenser heat,
    And weeds of worldly care.

"Though buried deep or thinly strewn,
    Do Thou Thy grace supply:
  The hope in earthly furrows strewn
    Shall ripen in the sky."

THE END.